The One-Eyed Sky

Also by Max Evans

Southwest Wind
Long John Dunn of Taos
The Rounders
The Hi Lo Country

Three Short Novels
by Max Evans

The Great Wedding

The One-Eyed Sky

My Pardner

1963
Houghton Mifflin Company Boston
The Riverside Press Cambridge

For Two Men of Books,
Norman Berg and Harold Torbert

The Great Wedding

One

He was at it again. Jim Ed Love was smooth-talking hell out of me and poor old Wrangler.

"Now, boys, I had a tough time gettin' you fellers out of that Hi Lo jail. Why you was charged with everything but rape, and if I hadn't seen the kind of gals you was courtin' I'da figured you guilty of that . . . drunk, disturbin' the peace, assaulting an officer of the law . . ." Then he rubbed his great big whey belly shaking that gold watch chain and said, like he was talking to a couple of runny-nose orphans, "Tch, tch."

I knew we were trapped. Everything he said was true and then some. He had picked up a bunch of hot checks and fixed it with the judge to get us sprung.

I looked down at little, squatty Wrangler where he stood on his bent-out legs picking his nose. Right at this minute I was wishing so hard my corns ached that old Wrangler was married to a rich woman, but it was head-hurting clear that getting him married was not going to be the easiest job I ever had. Like the town fellers say, "Where there's a will . . ." and it was the only way I could figure out to get away from Jim Ed and get me a decent job for once in my life.

Jim Ed interrupted my thinking with, "Now, fellers, I know you had a reasonably hard winter down at the lower camp, what with spending the whole year gatherin' wild cows and such. I know you missed out on a lot of fun around the ranch here — poker games in the bunkhouse, drinkin' bouts ever' other Saturday in Hi Lo. Well, that ain't goin' to be no more."

I was beginning to believe him till he started rubbing that sirloin-manufactured belly and caressing the brim of that cloud-white fifty-dollar hat.

"No siree, fellers — " He laid one diamond-covered hand out on my shoulder so heavy and friendly if I'd had a tail I'd have wagged it hairless. "No siree, you're going to stay within a day's ride of headquarters where you can be in on *everything*. Now, we're startin' the roundup in a few weeks. You boys know that's the highlight of the year — sort of the sugar in the coffee so to speak."

Well, guess what? That is right, we shook hands and agreed to stay on at the slave-driving JL Ranch. We walked out of the house feeling kind of numb. There in the back of the pickup was Old Fooler.

I said, "Wrangler, at least this'll give me a chance to get even with that good-for-nothing-but-trouble horse on my own terms. I don't mind the fact that he's tried to kill me ever' way known to horse, man and maybe God, but when he jumped the rail and lost us all that money in the horse race at Hi Lo, well, the right words are goin' beggin'."

Wrangler grunted out of his somewhat caved-in face and Old Fooler seemed to actually smile at me. It caused another one of them uneasy feelings, that smile. If he'd showed his teeth I would have known what to do — take a fence post and bust him between the ears.

As usual Jim Ed had a big, heavy calf crop that spring and all the other ranchers sent "reps" over for the fall roundup to see if any of their cattle were mixed in with the JL brand. There wasn't much time for visiting among old friends. Jim Ed saw to that. I will say one thing, he gave me and Wrangler the great honor of assigning us the outside circle. Now that is the longest and hardest ride and takes the best cowboys to handle it. I don't think that had much to do with what kind of cowboys we were but more to do with the long, hard ride.

They had a Dodge Power Wagon all rigged up like an old-time chuck wagon with a chuck box on the back and a cranky cook up front. Roundup was like Jim Ed said, "sugar in the coffee."

I mounted Old Fooler for the first circle and Wrangler roped him a brown out of the remuda. We worked up through the brush making a wide circle, jumping out little bunches of cattle now and then. We shoved them back down to the holding grounds on the flats. Old Fooler was working smooth and right. A cow no sooner tried to turn back than that old devil blue roan was biting her right in the rump.

By noon the horses were tiring so we rode back down to the remuda and roped two fresh mounts. I knew tomorrow we'd be working in rougher country and I wanted that crazy Fooler horse under me.

We rode back out for the brush under a sure enough blue sky. The grass on Jim Ed's outfit looked riper than yellow corn and thicker than hair on a skunk's tail. It was what is known among some thoughtful folks as a mighty fine fall day.

We reined up to roll ourselves a smoke and I said, "Wrangler, there comes a time in every cowboy's life when he needs to hang up his spurs for a spell. Sort of set in the saddle without movin', so to speak," and I gazed off into about nine hundred miles of space.

Wrangler grunted in what sounded to me like drunk Navaho and took a drag on his smoke that made her burn halfway to his jaws right before my eyes.

"Now for us old, broke-up cowboys they ain't too many choices."

He looked at me, those little rat-shaped eyes just asking "How?" right out loud.

"First, we can't draw none of this here unemployment pay. Cowboys ain't never had any of that. Second, it's mighty hard and costly to get insurance on a cowboy. So collecting that is next to impossible. Now we could go on relief. You know, get hungry enough a feller'll do anything."

"Oh, it's against the law to starve to death in this country," said Wrangler.

"How do you figger that?"

"Well, if you get so hungry and weak you cain't stand up, some damn fool will drag you in off the street and feed you."

This last, one of the longest speeches in history made by Wrangler, kinda defeated my purpose so I whipped up and got to the main point.

"Course a man could save all that embarrassment and injury to his pride by marrying a rich woman."

"That ain't easy," Wrangler said with great wisdom.

"Ain't nothin' easy," I said battling right back. "Besides a feller could do a lot of good in the world, like takin' care of his old bunged-up friends by givin' them good jobs on an easy-to-run outfit."

"Well, why don't you marry one?" said that dumb Wrangler.

I swallered hard and studied that nine hundred miles of space again, then I said, "I just ain't got the charm, that's all. If I had what you have, Wrangler, I'd of been hooked up years ago."

He sort of stiffened in the saddle and I could tell this last had taken hold. Course, if a man had to admit to who was the best looking between us, old Wrangler wouldn't even be sucking hind teat, he'd be dragging right by the end of the tail. But I figured it best to keep him thinking the other way.

Two

I DID some hard thinking. If I was going to get Wrangler married off the best thing to do was discourage him towards punching cows every way I could. So to start with, I make the widest circle that day I ever heard of. A cowboy may have a rawhide hind-end, but that won't keep it from getting numb.

That evening we finished filling up on beans and biscuits just as the sun turned off. Most of the boys hit their bedrolls early. Old Wrangler didn't even say goodnight.

The cook was cleaning up and the boys riding night herd out in the flats were wishing they were back in camp. I eased back on my bedroll and tried to think some more. I stared up at those zillion stars, nothing helped. It's pretty hard to think with a numb ass.

The next day we caught up our horses. Wrangler's had a hump in his back like a snake-bit hog. He saddled him, led him up a few steps and climbed on. The brown broke out in a dead run, swallered his head and went straight up about six feet. When he came down he hit the ground with all four feet bunched close together. I felt like my neck was broken just watching, but it didn't even seem to bother Wrangler because he just headed him off in the direction we were going to work.

I mounted up and followed. But just before I did, I grabbed a bottle of Hi-Life the cook used to get rid of stray dogs, and shoved it in my chaps pocket. By the time I caught Wrangler he had pulled the bronc's head up where it belongs.

"Feels good, don't he?"

Wrangler grunted.

We rode on a piece before the horse settled down enough so Wrangler would tear his hand away from the saddle horn.

"This here is some life, ain't it, Wrangler? Get up in the morning with nothing but smoke in your eyes to warm by. The coffee's so thick and bitter it tastes like cedar bark. The biscuits harder'n cinch rings and the bacon is salty and tooth-breakin' tough. Nice gentle horses, too. Easy on a man's old broken bones. You know what I heard the last time we were in Hi Lo?"

Grunt.

"Well, I heard that ever' time an old boy rode a bucking horse it meant one less drunk he could go on!"

He twisted his head around on his shoulders, staring with his eyes wide open. He didn't say anything but I could tell I'd penetrated to the quick.

The sun was up and shining on the mesas and we could see a few fresh tracks now. We reined up.

"Look," I said, pointing way off to the west, "ain't that

a bunch of cattle in that opening between them rock bluffs?"

He looked.

I slipped the Hi-Life out and poured it right plentifully on the root of his horse's tail. Now when you pour this stuff on a dog it soaks down around the hair roots and he will run a mile in two minutes, yapping his head off — and he won't be back to visit. It has a funny smell, something like chloroform, so I thought I'd talk fast and keep Wrangler's mind clean off this horse's intentions.

"Do you see 'em?"

"Naw."

"You sure?"

"Yaw."

Blooey! Away they went. Two jumps out and one back. Wrangler went east and the old pony south.

I took off after the horse feeling mighty sorry about Wrangler having to walk. I just wasn't going to let that happen to my best friend. Way up on the mesa I could hear brush popping and hoofs pounding against rock. It took me quite a spell to hem the brown up in a blind draw and catch him. Then I rode out in a patch of brush where I could look back down at Wrangler. He was up limping around, twisting his head one way and another trying to hear my return.

I sat there about an hour, real still, feeling it my duty to let Wrangler have a chance to get over his embarrassment.

When I finally rode up and said, "Feels good, don't he?" I thought Wrangler was going to choke on all the cuss words he was spitting out.

We finally moved several little bunches of cattle down towards the main herd.

It had been a hard day but nothing like the night. Breakfast came just after midnight it seemed to me. Old Wrangler was sure limping. Of course, he's not much of a walker at his best.

We rode out about a mile from camp when I got itchy to go on with my plans. But I was afraid to pull the cattle-spotting stunt again. Pretty soon old Wrangler pulled it for me. He thought he'd located some stock.

"Yeah," I said, "I believe that is a couple of head, but what is that spot off about fifty yards to the right?" Then I poured on the Hi-Life.

Before it could soak in, old Wrangler spurred up a couple of steps, yanked back on the reins and jumped off. Their heads went down together as Wrangler bit down on the horse's ear. That ole pony was shaking all over trying to make up his mind which end was hurting the most. Wrangler just held him there with his ear clinched between his teeth. After a while Wrangler turned loose and the Hi-Life effects must have been gone because the horse just kind of scooted around, snorted at Wrangler a couple of times and settled down.

I said, "What'n hell's the matter?"

"I ain't sure," he said, "but this ole pony smelled just like that one did yesterday."

We rode back to camp late that afternoon with me and Wrangler feeling just about the same, sort of let-down and mean as bloody-nosed bears.

We finished the roundup and all I could say when they hauled all those fat, profitable calves off to market in those big long red cattle trucks was, "It sure would be nice if those were yours, Wrangler. Just think, you could go on up to Denver with 'em and stay drunk all the time you was countin' your money."

"They ain't mine," he said.

I had to agree.

Three

OLD JIM ED sure hadn't lied to us. We could play poker any night we wanted with the boys in the bunkhouse. The trouble was, our hands were so bent and sore from lifting bales of hay we couldn't shuffle the cards.

Haying was a big thing on the JL. South of the house were acres and acres of hayfields, all irrigated from springs. Jim Ed always kept a lot of extra hay so he'd have it ready in case of a big blizzard. I'd heard that one winter he'd come into thousands of acres in Texas and Colorado by controlling the feed market, and made a fortune selling hay to stricken ranchers. Nice feller, our boss.

I really caught Jim Ed off guard when I volunteered mine and Wrangler's services for this hay gathering. Of course, Wrangler didn't know this and I decided it wasn't my place to tell him.

Now this hay was cut and crushed into bales weighing about eighty pounds apiece and there were thousands of them. We pitched bales all day long onto a flatbed truck, then we piled one on top of the other into a pyramid-shaped stack. This was just the first cutting. There'd be another for us later.

"Wrangler," I said, stopping to take a breath and a smoke, "if a man was married to a rich woman he wouldn't have to put up hay. As far as that goes his number one foreman wouldn't either."

"How come?"

"Why, we'd either hire it done or buy it from some other fool. A man needs to be in shape to rodeo and go dancin'. He shouldn't be gettin' out of trainin' by crackin' his back on this hay."

"Sounds fine," he said.

I was encouraged by his enthusiasm.

"Now soon as we get a couple of paydays together, I think we ought to go in and see Rosie at the General Mercantile. It's been two years since her old man died. She must be gettin' lonesome for some male company."

Grunt.

"Now think of this, Wrangler, she's got a big store paid for, a twenty-section ranch running along the main highway with plenty of improvements and water, and no tellin' what else."

"She ain't gonna marry no cowboy."

I hadn't thought about this part of it. It was true that Rosie had known at least three thousand broken-down, worthless cowboys in her time. We'd just have to figure a way to make old Wrangler appear different. I had plenty of time to think about it the next few days.

We put up the hay and I told Jim Ed on the sly that I felt me and Wrangler had had it too soft and wondered if he couldn't find us a fence-building job. He did the next morning.

One of his big springs had turned into a bog. Cows were commencing to get out in it and sink down so far they had to be roped and pulled out. It would take a strong fence to enclose it.

Now a posthole digger is a mighty mean-looking thing to get hold of just standing still, but when you raise the handles as high as you can reach and drive it into the hard ground all day long, it is something most cowboys won't even think of, much less talk about. After the holes are dug, the posts have to be lined up straight and tapped into the ground solid. Then you stretch the wire and staple it to the posts. On top of all that you build gates and hang deadmen (rocks tied to the corner post and buried in the ground) so it will stand upright.

It might be an interesting change of work for a rock-busting prisoner, but it was beginning to tell on us cowboys. This was what I wanted. I was willing to go through any sacrifice to show my friend the bright and sparkling righteousness of hooking up with a rich woman.

I said, "You got to admit that things would look better to us if you was roastin' your shins out at Rosie's ranchhouse knowin' that she was in town selling them beans and bacon, and your best friend was out in the pasture looking after your cattle. Why, right now instead of holding a bunch of blood blisters in both hands you could be caressin' a fat bottle of bourbon. Not only that but you could bed down tonight full of fine steak and whiskey right next to big-teated Rosie. As it is, you'll sleep in a cold bunkhouse full of cold, dirty cowboys."

"There's some difference there," Wrangler admitted.

Well I figured he was far enough along for me to make my real sales talk — the one I'd been studying over and saving up.

"Wrangler, if Old Fooler was a genuine gentle horse, one you could trust your life with . . ."

"Wouldn't even trust him with Jim Ed's life."

"I know, but what I mean, supposin' he *was* gentle."

"Yeah."

"Would you bet on him in a horse race against anything around Hi Lo?"

"Hell yes. Why?"

"I'll tell you why, because I've got a plan to make you look really right in Rosie's eyes. Not only that, but you'll appear to be the smartest cowboy this side of Canada."

"That's lots of country."

"You're a smart cowboy."

"How come?"

"Listen now, listen like you was goin' to be *given* a thousand dollars worth of Vince Moore's bootleg whiskey if you don't miss a word I say."

Four

I WAS STILL trying to explain things when we drove up in front of Vince Moore's house.

Now I'll say this for Vince's place: even if the windmill is generally broken, corral poles split and falling all over, panes out of half the windows, the chimney leaking smoke from a loose joint, the porch leaning way to the north, there is plenty of action — chickens scratching about and doing things all over the yard, dogs barking and wagging tails at the same time, dirty-faced kids peeking around the porch, the corner of the house, and between their mother's legs and Vince throwing the door to the outhouse open yelling, "Don't leave, boys. I'll finish in a breeze."

"Howdy, Mrs. Moore."

"What do you mean, 'Mrs. Moore'? Now, Dusty Jones, you know my name is Marthy."

"That I do, Marthy."

"Howdy, Marthy," said Wrangler.

"Why howdy, Wrangler Lewis," she said, pushing the straight cords of hair back behind her ears, and trying to shove her chest out and lift her suckling glands just a little. It was too late for that — round fifteen years too late. Kids just plain have a habit of swinging down on them instead of up, and when you've had as many kids as Marthy . . .

"Coffee?" she asked as we stepped inside, "Er . . . something else?"

"Something else sounds mighty fine to me," said Wrangler, suddenly snapping to.

She got some big tin cups from the cupboard, set them out in front of us and said Vince would be there in a minute to get the *goody* for us.

"What you boys been doin' besides Jim Ed's dirty work?"

"That's all, Marthy. That's all."

Wrangler nodded.

Jim Ed had been able to take over everybody's ranch that jogged into his but Vince's little outfit. He broke Vince as a cowman, but Vince had come on strong as a bootlegger — of course, strong to Vince might be weak to other people. If he had a new batch of whiskey made up, a half sack of beans and the same of flour he was pretty stable. Besides he liked chasing coyotes with his old skinny dogs better than he did cattle anyway.

Vince came busting through the door just knocking kids seven ways, shaking hands, pouring whiskey and talking like a radio all at once. He set the jug down on the table, threw a bunch of grease shaped like a hat on the floor and said, "It sure is good to see you. It sure is." Then his face sort of fogged over. He whammed his cup down and ran to the door. "I knew it," he yelled. "By god I knew it. The mean-eyed son of a bitch is still alive. You ain't tradin' him to me again! He tore up my corrals, fences, everything!" His hair had fallen down over his milky eyes but he was too mad to see anyway.

"Now calm down, Vince," I said. "Why, I wouldn't trade you that blazed-face roan for your whole outfit, kids and all."

Vince sorta whoa'd a minute, breathing like he had to and even if his eyes were covered I knew they were bugging.

"Liars, liars!" he said through clenched teeth as he glanced at Old Fooler standing peaceful-like in the back of the pickup. "I . . . I . . ."

"Now here, have another drink and listen to what we've thought up."

Vince's hair was kinda like Marthy's only thinner and rattier looking. I was glad when he pushed it out of his eyes so I could tell if it had come in his mind to grab the shotgun off the wall and blow my cockeyed head off.

"Here's the plan, Ever'body knows that Old Fooler can outrun anything in the country. He proved that last Fourth of July when he was leading the best horse around by four jumps."

"I tell you I wouldn't have that damn horse if you gave me Jim Ed's ranch to take him."

"Now, Vince, I ain't giving you no sales talk. Just listen." He poured us another drink while I went on, "At the same time ever'body knows that horse jumped the rail and had a runaway."

"We lost," said Wrangler.

"That's right, we lost," I agreed. "We lost ever'thing we'd won in the rodeo and a whole year's wages. Taking ever'thing into consideration I want to ask you boys a question."

"Shoot."

Wrangler said, "Uh."

"Will you fellers agree that you can depend on Old Fooler to mess up no matter what?"

"Hooray, hell yes, and I should say so right out loud in church," said Vince.

"Ever' goddamned time," said Wrangler.

"That's all I need to know," I said, smiling into my cup. "Now, I'm goin' to wind this up fast, so hang on and listen close."

Vince leaned forward across the table. Wrangler humped up with his cup stopped dead-still an inch from his mouth. That's listening, brother.

"Well, if Old Fooler was to suddenly turn black . . ."

"Oh good! You're goin' to kill him and let him rot," Vince said hopefully.

"Will you fellers let me do the talking. Now if he was to turn black on the outside . . . say that somebody rubbed some of that charcoal you use all the time to make this wonderful stuff we're drinkin' all over that roan, he'd turn black wouldn't he?"

"Blacker'n a bear's butt," said Wrangler snapping to a little more all the time.

"Blacker'n Jim Ed's heart," said Vince.

"Now, don't get carried away," said Marthy from over in the corner where she was patching a shirt.

"Now, if some folks around Hi Lo was to see this here beautiful black horse at a distance — just see him runnin' loose and free they would know he was a runnin' fool. Right?"

"Right."

"Right."

"All right, then. In that case if somebody was to match a race on that little bay of yours, Vince, then ever'body would bet on the black."

"Right, by god."

"Whoopeee," Wrangler agreed strongly.

I stopped for breath and poured us all another cup of that perfect thirst quencher from the crock jug.

"If we was to have five hundred dollars bet on the bay we would be sure to win, huh?"

"Couldn't miss," said Vince, "because that Old Fooler horse would jump the rail, fall down, start bucking or running the wrong way before you'd get a quarter of the way around the track."

"Well, me and Wrangler here ain't been to town, Vince, in several paydays, and we've got her right here in cash!" I threw it all out on the table, and Vince tried to swaller the tin cup.

"Now all you got to do is co-operate a little and we'll clean out that Hi Lo so fast it won't know what county it's in."

On the way over to Vince's I told Wrangler that if we'd

tip Rosie off so she'd get down some good fat bets, she would sure appreciate the winnings. Not only that, but she'd just bust her big, fat drawers wanting to marry old Wrangler when I told her it was *all* his idea. A smart man like that is hard to find.

Vince stood up and sloshed out another round.

"Dusty, you're a go-gettin' son of a bitch!"

"Wrangler," I asked, feeling kind of embarrassed at all that praise, "what do you think?"

"Whatever suits you just tickles me plumb to death."

I knew from past experiences I had Wrangler sold to the gut hollow.

Five

WE GOT Old Fooler out of the pickup. It wasn't easy to do, but with the help of Vince's jug we got her done. Vince brought out a keg of charcoal and we started rubbing it on him.

"Ain't that purty?" I said.

"Yeah," said Wrangler.

"It ain't gonna stay put, fellers," said Vince.

"It don't have to stay long," I said.

"Just long enough to clean out Hi Lo," said Wrangler.

Right there, I, Dusty Jones, started using this head of mine for smart purposes again. I never felt so cockeyed smart in my whole life.

"Vince?"

"Yeah, Dusty."

"You got any varnish?"

"Sure have, by doggies, a whole gallon of it. Had it for years. Been aimin' to use it on somethin' like the floor or maybe a wagon bed."

"Your problems are over."

"How's that?"

"Just get it, Vince. Just bring it to old Dusty."

While Vince went to get the varnish I went back in the house to see Marthy on important business.

"Marthy, do you have a fly sprayer?"

"Yeah, but we ain't had any ammunition for it in three years. Flies ain't bad out here anyway, not enough fer 'em to eat."

"Well, let me borrow it for just a spell."

She handed it over.

"Now, boys, watch this," I said as I poured the varnish in the flysprayer. They sure did watch.

Then I reared back and mashed the handle with the machine aimed right at Old Fooler. Nothing happened. I tried her again. The same.

"It's too thick," I said, and grabbed the jug away from Wrangler. He put up quite a fight till I explained I was only going to use a shot or two.

I poured half the varnish out of the spray and filled it up with whiskey. Then I gave her a good shaking and mashed that handle again. The trick was done. That stuff sprayed out of there and settled the charcoal down just like it had grown that way.

"By god, fellers," old Vince said, "I done said it, that Dusty's a go-gettin' son of a bitch!"

I didn't even have time to agree. I said, "Get your bay horse, Vince, we're headin' for Hi Lo."

Wrangler said, "Whooooopeee and hurrah," and jumped just as high as he could right straight up in the air. At that he just barely got off the ground.

We crowded both horses in the pickup bed, Vince fetched another jug and we all yelled goodbye at Marthy and the kids. When they answered back it sounded like a jail full of drunks. Away we went.

Just before getting into Hi Lo we turned off down a little wagon road and hunted some brush. We unloaded the horses. I tied Old Fooler with a double catch-rope to a stout cedar.

"Now, Vince, give me and old Wrangler about an hour in town. Then you come ridin' in like you hadn't seen us in a year. You know what to do from there on."

"Sure do," he said. "Here, fellers, give me that jug. It's gonna get lonesome out here the next hour."

When times were better, Hi Lo had several saloons. Now there were just two, the Double Duty and the Wildcat. It didn't take a man long to make up his mind. Today we picked Nick Barnes' Wildcat.

"Well, looky here," he said, "if it ain't Dusty and Wrangler. Ain't seen you boys since the Fourth of July."

"We ain't been anywhere to be seen," I said.

"Whiskey," Wrangler said.

"Whiskey," I said.

"Comin' up. Doubles or singles?"

"One of each," I said.

"Too bad the way that old roan horse double-crossed you in that race, Dusty. You boys could have bought old Jim Ed's whole outfit with those winnings."

"Well, I ain't aimin' to lose another." I wanted to thank Nick for bringing up the right subject at the right time. I ordered us another drink figuring that was thanks enough for any bartender.

Then I went on, "I've got a black horse, gentle as an old blind dog, but faster than that Old Fooler horse ever thought about."

"Is that a fact?" Nick said, wiping the sweat off his forehead and rubbing spilled whiskey on his hatbox belly.

"That's a fact."

Wrangler said, "I don't believe he's that fast myself."

"Now, Wrangler, I've told you and told you that I've run him against Old Fooler and it was a dead heat."

"That's good enough for me," said Nick.

"Sure wish somebody'd come along with some sporting blood," I said, and in a few minutes somebody with that very kind of blood rode up singing and yelling to beat hell. I'll be damned if it wasn't Vince Moore.

"Wonder what he's doin' in town?" I said.

"Looks drunk to me," said Nick.

"Naw, just headin' that way," said Wrangler.

It didn't take Vince long to tie that good-looking bay to a telephone pole, come in and have three drinks on me and Wrangler. In the time it takes to do that very thing a bunch of people had started to gather. Delfino Mondragon was in town with six months' back pay from sheep herding. Cowboys, farmers and all, gathered around knowing there was something going to happen. It did.

Delfino said, "Dusty, I feels like a leetle poker game."

He rubbed his black Mexican hair and said again, "A leetle games of chances."

Vince Moore whammed his glass down and said, "I'll

match that bay horse right there, for five-eighths of a mile, against any horse in the country!"

I said, "Why, Vince, I've got an old black horse that is just havin' a fit to run. In fact, if he don't get hisself in a race soon I figger he's just goin' to fret his poor self to death."

"I'm gonna give you the opportunity to save a horse's life. Cause I'll bet five hundred he cain't run as good as you think he can."

Well, all hell and things that were more fun broke loose. Everybody wanted to see this black.

I said, "Now just a minute, boys. When the time is right I'll have him ready. But first let's toast Hi Lo and all the fine people around it. To all the rich and all the poor, and let's go ahead and say that we hope some of them folks get to change places now and then, so they'll know how the other side feels."

I was so damn near out of breath it took me about a minute to tell Wrangler, "Get over to Rosie's and tip her off!"

Out he scooted.

Now old Vince had our five hundred and he was willing to bet it for us. Every dollar of it was to go on the bay.

As soon as I saw Wrangler and Rosie Peabody standing on the porch of the mercantile, I said, "Now, fellers, all of you line up down at the race track bleachers and I'll show you that black."

A big yell went up and everybody headed for the track. I took off for the brush. I saddled Old Fooler and told him, "Now, I've given you a reprieve from soap factories. I've kept you from being turned into dog food time after time. Now's your opportunity to pay me back. Just don't buck till I turn you loose at full speed."

Old Fooler looked at me and it was almost a kind expression that came on his face. I picked up the nearly empty jug Vince had left and settled its fate in one swaller. I had confidence.

As I rode out onto the track, the black hair gleamed where the varnish was on it. In the late fall like this, the other horses around had started putting on long winter hair. This black looked like he'd been combed and prepared for the Kentucky Derby. When we headed down the track I opened Old Fooler up, but at the same time I didn't let a millionth of an inch of slack come in the reins. If I had he'd have thrown me clear over the bleachers. That's exactly what I wanted him to do later.

As soon as I got around the track, where nobody could get close enough to examine Old Fooler, I looked over at the crowd. I could just hear them sucking in their breaths at this beautiful-moving, shiny race horse. They were all gathered around Rosie and Vince making bets. I knew the odds had jumped a mile as soon as they saw the horse. I circled once more holding him back.

Vince rode out and we lined up a little ways back from the bleachers. It was agreed that Rosie would say *go*. She gave me a big wink right out over them big teats Wrangler would enjoy so much, and I could feel my shins roasting by her fireplace already. I could just see Wrangler getting up around ten in the morning and saying,

"Dusty, some time this month we've got to get out and look for a stray cow." Why, after this race he would actually be able to buy and pay for the wedding ring. Wonderful, wonderful world!

"Go!"

We did.

I have been on some fancy-moving things in my life when you figure it all the way around, but it seemed like Old Fooler was going to outdo them all. He sure did. He passed the bay so fast I didn't have time to wave goodbye. When we hit the first turn, I pitched him the slack. I knew he would take rail and all when he left the track. Well, I damn near fell off because I was expecting to go one way but he kept running the other. *That* is right. Straight down the middle of the track we went.

Well at the end of the five lengths he was way, way ahead. But that was nothing, on his second time around he caught up with the bay from behind. Then, *that,* is right, *then* he jumped the fence.

He was beginning to slow down some when we hit Shorty Wilson's back yard. I'm sure glad it wasn't fenced. I could see a clothesline full of diapers coming right at us. I yanked on the reins as hard as I could and spurred even harder on one shoulder trying to turn him. It did. It turned him from a runner to a bucker. I ain't sure he meant to do it but he saved my life right there. That clothesline would have cut me right in half but Old Fooler, bless his heart, jumped so high that he hung the saddle horn over it and when he came down the line broke at both ends. I reached down trying to get hold of the horn, but it was too late. I prolonged fate about six or seven more jumps and away I went.

As soon as I could get the gravel brushed out of my eyes I looked up to see where Old Fooler was headed. That black-ass bastard was headed uphill for heaven, with two wings of wet diapers flapping the breeze.

It was almost dark before we finally caught Old Fooler and got him loaded in the pickup with the bay and the rest of us. I didn't ask Wrangler how Rosie felt, I knew. I didn't ask Vince how he felt, I knew. There was one of those silences that only the deaf can know.

We hit the highway and I thought it best to bypass town because Shorty Wilson's wife might want her diapers back and it would take me twenty-five years to gather them.

Finally Vince said, "You know what?"

"What?" old blabbermouth Wrangler asked.

"That Fooler horse is a go-gettin' son of a bitch!"

Six

I CAN TELL YOU one thing for sure, Jim Ed would just naturally see to it that we got in plenty of work. But old cunning me — I decided to help things along. The way I figured it, old Wrangler just had to get sure enough fed up with this ranch life, at least on the hired hand's end, before he'd get serious about marrying a rich woman.

A second hay cutting was about ready so I bobbed up and volunteered our best efforts. Now Jim Ed acted kind of surprised, but he acted a little bit tickled, too. It ain't the easiest thing in the world to get a couple of broke-up cowboys to put up hay twice in one year.

We took to riding a tractor; that is right. Hard to believe, but sure as hell true. Hooked to that tractor was a long hay-cutting blade that sliced her down slick. Then we came along and raked it up into wind rows and let it dry a couple of days in the hot sun. After that we drove a hay baler over it and the next thing you knew the fields were covered with pretty green bales.

Getting that hay into bales is just the first item; the second ain't quite so easy. It has to be loaded on a flat-bed truck, hauled to the stack lots, unloaded and stacked bale by bale in the form of a long pyramid. Lift. Lift. Lift. It takes some doing. Me and Wrangler were the doers.

After about two weeks of this I could tell my pardner was beginning to weaken. It was also getting boring do-ing the same thing over and over. That's just the way I wanted it. He even started talking *first* for once.

"This here work ain't fit for nothin' but mules," he said.

"You're right," I agreed.

"Well, how come we're doin' it then?"

I came right back at him since the whole thing was my bright idea, "Mules are too smart."

He grunted once and farted twice as he lifted a great big bale up to me on the stack.

We stacked right on into winter. And I might say there were times when I felt a little bit stupid for getting into this myself.

When we finished the hay-stacking, it was getting cold —plenty cold. In fact, we had washed and hung out a bunch of levis to dry and when Wrangler went to gather them in he had to turn them all upright to get through the bunkhouse door. He just leaned them up against the wall like sticks until they thawed out.

I slipped over to Jim Ed's that night and had a little talk.

"Jim Ed," I said, hoping his wife wouldn't come in the living room and examine my boots for foreign matter, as the town fellers say, "a lot of them posts around the stack lots are rotted so bad a feller cain't tighten the wires. If it comes a bad blizzard the cattle are just liable to walk right through that fence and tear down all them haystacks."

"You don't say?"

"Sure do."

"Well, Dusty, I'll put a couple of the odd-job boys on it right away."

"No need for that, Jim Ed, just sic me and old Wrangler on it."

He looked at me kinda sly-like and said, "Well, all right, but hadn't you rather ride fence, drive a truck and feed, or something a little more suitable for saddle-raised men?"

"No," I said, "by god you've saved me and Wrangler from goin' to jail and I'm goin' to see that we take on ever' dirty job you've got around here till we're even."

"Suits me," he said.

We had a couple of long iron bars and a couple of posthole diggers. I might as well say it now that I wanted to back out before the first day was over. The ground was already frozen down about eighteen inches as solid as Wrangler's skull. That meant that it took about an hour to bite out the first half of the hole and about two minutes for the rest. They had to be almost three feet deep to hold right. It was like digging in cement, and the unhandy part about posthole diggers, as I've mentioned before, is the fact that you have to pick them up every time you drive them at the ground. Otherwise they don't dig. Now if the soil hadn't been so rocky we could have used the automatic posthole digger on the back of Jim Ed's tractor. But if that had been the case I'd never have volunteered in the first place.

Our hands got a permanent bend in them. They looked just like hay hooks. It would take four or five gallons of Vince Moore's whiskey before I could pick up anything bigger around than an apple.

One day Wrangler tried to roll a cigarette. He finally gave up and just turned the sack up in his mouth and started chewing. He ain't so dumb sometimes at that.

Then it sure enough got cold. The ground was frozen plumb to the bottom of those holes.

"Progress we ain't makin', Wrangler. All we're doin' is wearin' out some good iron bars and posthole diggers."

He tried to answer but all I saw was a bunch of frost come out of his mouth. His little old razor-back eyes were watering so fast they looked like two fresh bullet holes in a bucket of water.

Jim Ed finally saw the waste and gave us another job. An indoor job at that.

"Now by god," I told Wrangler, "ain't we the two luckiest bastards this side of Hi Lo and the other side of hell?"

"It's all in the way you look at it," said Wrangler bitterlike.

That's what I wanted him to say. It's all that gave me the courage to carry on.

Now Jim Ed has got some mighty big barns. On different occasions, such as blizzards or heavy rains, during calving season, he keeps cattle in these same barns. He also feeds these cattle to keep them strong and healthy. There was soon no doubt in my mind but what they were healthy. That is as far as constipation was concerned. I'm flat-ass certain that Jim Ed never owned a cow that was bothered with this. In fact, after me and Wrangler had worked in the barns awhile I'd have bet my last saddle blanket that they all had the thin dirties.

Jim Ed had said the barn was big and airy. This was true. There was so much air and it got so full of manure dust that a feller had a hard time getting a fresh breath. We backed a truck into the barn and started out digging and shoveling.

Wrangler said, "This stuff is froze just like the rest of the world."

"Yeah," I said, "but it'll break off in layers." It did, by the millions.

One of us was swinging the pick while the other was swinging that scoop shovel full of frozen you-know-what on the back of a truck. When that truck had all it could handle one of us would drive down across the pastures and the other would scatter it out behind. Jim Ed said this fertilized the pastures. I figured the cows would have done a better job of it than we did.

Now Wrangler wasn't exactly complaining. It was more just stating facts. But it gave me hope.

"Dusty," he said, standing there with a scoop shovel full of fertilizer.

"Yeah?"

"Jim Ed lied."

"He did?"

"Yeah, he said it'd be warmer in here. Hell's fire the sun don't never shine in here."

"Well, I think you misunderstood him, Wrangler. He said we'd be indoors out of the wind and weather. And that's true."

He grunted.

Several months and millions of shovels later he stopped, holding the shovel in the same half-ready position and said, "Dusty."

"Yeah?"

"It's damn near spring and you know what we've been doin' for a livin' nearly all winter?"

I knew all right. I stopped and tried to see out of my blurry eyes, over my runny nose and fought to keep that hellacious taste from getting any further down my throat than it was. Just the same I said, "What?"

"Shit," he said, swinging the shovel kinda mad-like. "We're makin' a livin' shovelin' shit."

I could hear them wedding bells ringing clear as a police siren in spite of the half inch of you-know-what packed in each ear.

Hope had calved again.

Seven

YES SIR, things were looking up. The grass was sprouting green and tender, the birds were telling everybody about it, and Wrangler, like all the other animals on earth, had his mind on love. On top of that we'd soon be working the spring roundup and branding — having some real fun.

Then it happened. Jim Ed came snorting and blowing up in front of me and said, "That goddamn horse! That goddamn horse!"

"What goddamn horse?" I said, feeling the question unnecessary but doing my best to be polite.

"That Old Fooler. Who else?" he said, jabbing a finger about the size of a pool cue in my chest. "He's run off with five of my best thoroughbred quarter horses!"

"Five?"

"Five!"

"How'd he get out of the big horse pasture?"

"Opened the gate hisself," said Jim Ed.

"He wouldn't do that," I said, swallering my Adam's apple as fast as it jumped up.

"Naw," Wrangler said, not helping much.

"He sure did," Jim Ed said, "and he's gone into the wild horse country. You know damn well I aimed to show all those horses at the state fairs in Dallas and Albuquerque and the Grand National in Denver next January. That son of a bitch will cripple them horses till they won't be fit for coyote bait. That is if we ever get 'em back. Get 'em back," he said again and raised his great big buttermilk belly almost even with the third button on his vest. "You'll get 'em back or no pay, no town, no nothing."

Well just when things looked good, like I might get Wrangler in town while it was still spring and we had several months back pay to boot, and give us a chance to hunt up that rich woman, Old Fooler had sure enough fouled up our world. I might say this was not unusual, just disappointing.

Jim Ed went on, "Now, you're going to be held responsible for them five horses. By the time you work 'em out you'll be a hundred and ten years old."

This was not a good thing to hear. Me and Wrangler were trapped again. It was none of our doing, but there wasn't a lawyer in the whole damn state would take our case against Jim Ed Love. That's the way lawyers are. And even if we had won the case, the judge would have ruled in Jim Ed's favor no matter what. The power's where the money is and me and Wrangler were short as hell on that last item. Besides, everybody knows money's more important than people.

Another thing I knew bothered Jim Ed about those horses, it was his way of showing off, keeping his name on people's tongues and being a big shot all over the Southwest. He liked to read in the paper: Sammy Bar, registered quarter horse owned by Jim Ed Love of Hi Lo, New Mexico, Wichita Falls, Texas, and Stony Stump, Colorado, takes grand prize blue ribbon.

Now I can't say as how I blamed Jim Ed for that, but from my viewpoint I would like to see the name Wrangler Lewis shoved in that sentence at the right place.

As of now it was going to take some doing to get her done.

Now ordinarily Jim Ed would have made us camp out on the hard ground while we tried to gather those horses, but this time it was different. Jim Ed was going to lose face if he didn't show up at those scheduled horse shows. If I hadn't had love and marriage on my mind so strong, I would've spent the rest of my life hunting those horses just to mess up Jim Ed. As it was he let us have the pickup and all the saddle horses we could use.

Every morning we got up before daylight, caught our horses, loaded them in the pickup and drove about six miles into wild horse country. Then we mounted and rode our hind ends plumb raw (and that is hard to do with a cowboy's hind end) looking for signs of those strays.

There were only about twenty-five wild horses left up in the brush, and with Old Fooler and Jim Ed's five that made a little over thirty. Now figuring that they were scattered over something like fifty thousand acres, and figuring that there are one hundred and fifty trees to the acre — not counting all the bushes under them — it don't take no town feller to savvy that the odds were against us.

Every once in a while we would jump a little bunch. Away we'd go tearing through timber, ducking tree limbs (part of the time), dodging holes and crevices, and piling up over big rocks. We were working down lots of saddle horses and getting nowhere.

After about three weeks of this I told Wrangler, "Now, we've finally got Old Fooler's range located and we know where they're watering most of the time."

"Yeah," he said, humping up in the saddle and pushing his hat back.

"So, let's build a wild horse trap around the most used waterhole."

Old Wrangler said for an answer, pushing his hat back, "That sure is a skinny cloud up there."

I pushed *my* hat back and looked, "That ain't no cloud, that's a vapor trail."

"You mean there's a bird that leaves a trail in the sky?"

I just couldn't believe he was that dumb. On the other hand, he'd spent his whole life looking at the ground for cattle and horse sign. And this was the first time I could recall Wrangler looking at the sky. All he'd ever got from up there in the heavens was a leather-scorching sun, high winds and freezing blizzards. I gave him the benefit of the doubt and told him about jet airplanes.

"Oh," he said, and I couldn't tell whether he believed me or not.

Well, we built a wild horse trap that would have made

the best carpenter in the world proud of us. It was eight feet tall, the wire stretched tight as a whore's girdle, and the bottom two wires set back so we'd have a place to scramble to if the horses went on the prod. We covered this all over with heavy brush so you couldn't see the wire leaning on it. Then we swung the gate open and covered it just as good but with lighter material. We were pleased.

We hunted and we hunted. Twice we saw Old Fooler for a minute as he led the horses out of sight into the badlands. We were both peeled and bruised from top to bottom. And I might add our tempers were in the same shape.

Then the insult of all insults took place. It appeared to me to be as dirty as if somebody had slipped President Kennedy a mickey just before he spoke to the nation. Jim Ed called his Texas ranch for an airplane. They used them down there to scare cattle out of the brush. Not only that, but Jim Ed said we would have to pay for the pilot's time and gasoline. This was damn near too much.

Now our job, according to Jim Ed, was to stay up on a hill kind of concealed from sight as far as the horses were concerned and wait until this airplane drove them down into our trap, then we were to dash bravely down and close the gate. That sounded real fine, but so does a church bell at a funeral.

For three days we hunkered down holding our horse's reins, watching that tin bird fly around the hills.

"Now, ain't that something," I said, "a flying cowboy. I never thought the time would come I'd have to even get in the same county with one of them things. God-uh-mighty, the world's ruined, Wrangler. You ain't goin' to allow that on your ranch, are you?"

"Hell no," he said, "I'd chop the wings off that damn thing and make an outhouse out of it."

That was the way I liked to hear my pardner talk. Just then I damn near died. Here came that hombre and right under him was Old Fooler and a bunch of horses. The plane circled, sounding like a runaway rock crusher. But just when he was bending her in to shove them into the corral, Old Fooler turned and headed right up the side of a steep hill.

Now this is where the remains of the Wild and Woolly West brought sudden defeat to the modern age. That cow-pilot turned his plane and tried to climb in the air after Old Fooler. He topped out just behind him, but something got in his way. Two pine trees. The wings ripped off to each side and what was left of the plane rammed into a thick clump of oak brush and everything was out of sight — horses and all.

We rode over almost as fast as we could. I think if I'd hit my horse with the spurs just once we could have speeded things up. But me and Wrangler are both very tenderhearted cowboys and we never take advantage of dumb animals — just dumb people.

"By God he ain't dead," I said as I saw this pilot crawling out of the splintered plane.

"Oh hell," Wrangler said, then he corrected it when the pilot looked at us with spinning eyes. "Oh, hell is no place for airplane pilots."

"Where am I?" he asked.

"Well, now, I'll tell you, feller, you're a long ways from where you ought to be."

"Correct," Wrangler said.

"Shall we take him in or wait till Jim Ed comes after him, Wrangler?"

"Whatever suits you just tickles me plumb to death."

I knew he meant it, so I helped the pilot on behind the saddle and we started the first stages of delivering the lost to the fold. We found out that a cow-pilot's ass is not as tough as a cowboy's.

But I learned something that eased my pain a little bit. That plane was insured, so old Jim Ed couldn't make us pay for that, too. The way I looked at it we had saved the price of an airplane that day. That's lots of money even to bartenders and bank clerks. Oh, for the wild free life of a cowboy!

We kept right on hunting, and Jim Ed left us alone for a spell. Besides he and all the other hands were having a big time down at the spring roundup and branding.

Then it began to rain. Those black clouds built a roof over the mountains and sprung a leak. It rained enough to run an ocean over. It took us three hours to drive up to the hills with chains on the pickup and two to drive back home. That meant we had just a little over two hours a day to hunt wild horses. That's not much time in this big country.

The horses were slipping and sliding all over. A preacher uncle of mine told me he saw it rain so hard in California that a strong man could row a boat straight up in the air. I called him a liar. Now I wish he was here so's I could apologize.

"Wrangler, I didn't know a man could breathe water, did you?"

"There's lots of things a man can do we don't know about."

This wisdom was way over my head, so I shut my mouth before I drowned. I knew we were really in for it now. There would be water holes everywhere. Our chances of trapping that bunch of horses were about the same as a cowboy getting rich. Those are mighty long odds.

I decided since we were going to have to leave the JL without our pay, and since the cause of it was Old Fooler, that I'd shoot the low-lived son of a bitch. I started carrying a .30-30 on the saddle for that purpose.

Then the clouds busted up and the sun came dropping down on the land. The grass was stretching up and our backs drying out.

The fourth clear day, we rode up on a canyon so deep it must've been the roof to hell. And down in the bottom something was moving. After a long hard look we agreed that it appeared to be Old Fooler with a bunch of his slaves tagging behind. They were moving towards a shallower part of the canyon and towards our trap.

I said, "Let's ride like hell and get up ahead of 'em. They have to come out within a quarter mile of the trap. If we can't booger them into it I'll at least get a shot at that rottenhearted bastard of a roan horse."

Wrangler grunted.

We rode like hell. The wind was in our favor. We

waited and waited a whole bunch more. Then old Wrangler just pointed. His jaws were working silently like a single stem of grass in a high wind. I looked where he looked. My jaws worked, too. Old Fooler was slowly, as if it was his everyday job, leading that bunch into the trap. He walked right on in lazy-like. The others kinda hesitated, heads up, ears forward, snorting and trembling but they followed him in.

Well, old kindhearted us fairly shoved the steel in our horses' sides. I headed for the gate itself and Wrangler for the opening. We had a downhill run but even so four head broke out on us. But when the gate was shut tight we counted up and there besides Old Fooler and Jim Ed's five head were seven wild ones.

Old Fooler stood sleepy-like out in the middle with his eyes half closed. The rest just ran, and jumped and farted and turned like a bunch of airplane cowboys would've done. Plumb foolish-acting animals.

It took us quite a spell to rope each and every one of those seven wild ones and put a garter on them. (That is, we twisted a piece of rope so tight on one leg it cut off most of the circulation.) A three-legged horse is easier to drive. Then we turned them out and headed in. We left the pickup there. We could get it later.

It was damn near dark when I turned into the home gate with Old Fooler coming along nicely right behind and all the other horses scattered out between Fooler and Wrangler. Jim Ed was amazed. It was hard on him but he admitted the seven extra head would take care of everything.

We had a good night's sleep and he even sent another cowboy after the pickup. Then he paid us off the next morning.

We stuck the money in our pockets, loaded Old Fooler in the back of our own pickup and headed for a wedding. We didn't say goodbye to Jim Ed Love, but I sorta waved my fingers out in front of my face as we passed headquarters.

Eight

OLD WRANGLER really fought his head to get me to stop in Hi Lo.

He said, "I want a drink."

"That, I can understand."

"Well, stop."

"Cain't do'er, Wrangler."

"No brakes?" he asked, looking at the floorboard.

"No time," I said, "we got to get into Ragoon before night. We've done wore our welcome out in Hi Lo, and besides there ain't no rich women available since Rosie has deserted us."

Wrangler saw the truth of this, but he was still plenty thirsty.

Now nearly every time I'd been in town since I was eighteen years old I'd either been drunk, in a fight, in jail, or gone broke. Sometimes all four. It was all done in the interest of having fun, even though other folks

seemed to think different. But for once I was going to
try to handle these situations a little better — really use
my thinker. I knew we had to get a pretty fancy hotel to
meet rich women. That expense was okay, but this idea
of gambling and giving all our money away the first day
was out. Why, if we were careful, we could last a whole
month and that ought to get the job done. Another thing
that always set us back was those damn jails. It didn't
matter how you got in, whether it was your fault or not
the judge was going to say *guilty,* and fine you all the law
allowed. That was considerable.

"You know, Wrangler, we had a hell of a time collectin'
our wages," I said cautiously.

"Jim Ed's the *takin'* kind."

"That's what I meant. Now, when this is gone we may
never get that big amount together again."

"It ain't likely."

"So, we got to be careful till you find that everloving
woman with the big, fat purse."

He grunted.

I drove on, and then I saw the place. I knew it had to
be the one. There it was, off the road a piece. And it said,
COCKTAIL (I knew this was fancy talk for whiskey);
PHONE (no need for them far as I could tell); TV (hell,
Jim Ed had one of those but I'd never got to watch it);
SWIMMING POOL (might come in handy for sobering up
and taking a bath); DINING ROOM (kinda nice to have
in an emergency). Yes sir, the RAGOON INN had it all.
Not only that, it was plumb out on the edge of town so
there was lots of scrub oak and cedar to tie Old Fooler
until we could find somebody to pawn him off on.

I signed up for both of us at the register and paid a whole week in advance. The lady gave me a key and pointed out the room.

The Ragoon Inn was a big, old place made out of adobe bricks and there was so much glass in the main building two hundred people could have looked out all at once.

We drove the pickup out back and unloaded Old Fooler. Then we tied him to the pickup and gave him some oats. We'd have to feed and water the bastard every day until Wrangler got his marrying arrangements made — that is, unless we were lucky and he choked to death or something.

Then we went over to our room. It was the fanciest damn thing you ever saw. Two great big old beds, green rugs, just like a cow pasture after a good rain, a bathtub, a phone and one of them TV sets. There was a picture on the east wall of a naked lady standing there looking at a lake full of water. I walked over real close and took a better look but the woman was still too far off to tell much about her features.

Wrangler said, "Let's go get a drink."

"Not till we take a bath," I said, "and get on some clean clothes."

"I cain't wait," said Wrangler, and I could tell he meant it.

"Wait here just a minute," I said, "I'll go get us a bottle."

It was all right to get a little drunk the first night here but to be dirty and drunk both was not going to better our chances of starting a romance.

I went to the bar and brought back a bottle. Old

Wrangler was glad to see it. I guess this marrying idea had him a little upset. He took a big drink and said, "Ahhh." I could see that I was going to have to pioneer on this bath deal.

It didn't take me long. I'm a fast bath-taker. I ran a tub full of water for Wrangler. He took another slug of hooch, undressed and dived in.

"Wowwweeee, oh, oh, woowee."

I ran in to see what was the matter. I must have got the water a little hot. Old Wrangler was about to drown and it looked like when he got in he'd slipped and driven his big toe into the water faucet. I pulled his toe out and threw him out on the floor so he could get his breath. He was getting plenty of that, in fact the way he was choking and going on I believe he was getting too much air. His toe was all bloody and bent. I ran and handed him the bottle, feeling I had done my duty and more. Wrangler was going to be a problem.

I put on clean levis and a new shirt and told him, "I'm goin' on over to the bar. Come on over when you get ready."

I went up to the bartender and said, "A double," then I remembered my idea on making that money last and I said, "No, I'm too dry for that. Give me a beer."

He was a friendly feller with a belly as big as Jim Ed's but with a hell of a lot pleasanter look on his round, flat face. He smiled and said, "Whatever suits you is my pleasure."

I looked real hard at him a minute to see if he was kin to Wrangler. He talked some like him, but I knew he wouldn't admit it if he was.

I went over to the jukebox. Sure enough there was my favorite by Banjo Bill but I played some of those tunes by that Sinatra feller. I decided that was the kind of music old Wrangler ought to get married to. Then I got me a seat at a table halfway between the jukebox and the bar at a great big table. That beer was so good and that Sinatra feller so romantic-sounding that I plumb forgot about Wrangler, the time, and everything else. All of a sudden the jukebox went off and I threw my head up and there was a three-piece orchestra scattered out there on a little platform.

One of them started pounding hell out of a drum, another did the same to a piano and one of them was blowing into a horn with a lot of latches on it. It wasn't as good as that Sinatra feller but it wasn't bad either.

Then I realized the place was damn near full of people. I wanted to get up and go get Wrangler, but I was afraid I'd lose my table. I told the waitress just to bring me three beers so I wouldn't have to move for a spell. Time passed.

Then the waitress came up to my table followed by some women. Four of them to be exact.

"Could these ladies use your table? We're crowded. Miss Hopwell has a party of four."

I jumped up and started to run.

Miss Hopwell (I could tell she was the ringleader) said, "No, please, sit down. We'll just *join* you."

I plunked myself back down. Miss Hopwell pulled a coyote hide or something furry from around her neck and leaned forward. Her bosom slid out on top of the table like a couple of well-watered cantaloupes. If she'd been two inches shorter she couldn't have got within a foot of that table.

"I'm Miss Hopwell, Myrna Hopwell," she said. "And this," she said pointing a finger just plumb overloaded with rings, "is my niece Gloria, and these are her friends from college, Miss Devers and Miss Rollaway."

I nodded and said, "Howdy. I'm Dusty Jones."

"How is it you're called Dusty?" Miss Rollaway asked, rolling great big, green eyes like a hungry calf at a full bag of milk.

"I don't know," I said, "maybe it's because I'm such a fast bather."

They all laughed to beat hell. I had been dead serious, but it didn't take me long to find out two things about town women, they either sneer or laugh no matter what you say. This bunch was laughing. I tried to tell them about one of my uncle's dogs that thought he was a horse and ate grass till he starved to death. They laughed so damn hard I decided to shut up and dance. I asked Miss Rollaway first.

She was a mighty fine dancer, just snuggling up like a rubber hose and sliding round so easy I could hardly feel her touch the floor. Old Dusty was enjoying himself.

"Are you really a cowboy?" she asked, "I mean *really.* You dress like one, but so many people do, you know."

"Well, Miss Rollaway . . ."

"Jane," she said, and so did I.

"Jane, it's like this. If I said I was I'd be telling the truth, but if I said I was I'd be lying, too."

"I don't understand."

"Well, I used to be a fair hand and I reckon I could have been called some kind of a cowboy. You see, there just ain't no use for us anymore. They've got jeeps and airplanes, and tractors and pickup trucks," and I just went on and on.

"Oh," she said, "I think I understand."

I was glad she was a smart girl and had enough sense to shut up and dance. I danced with them all. Though I might say Myrna was somewhat of a problem. The way she was put together kind of made it impossible to scrunch up and get going. She was almost as tall as I was and I'm just about six feet.

I was doing my best when I heard a yell blast out across the dance floor that could come from only one person — Wrangler Lewis.

It wasn't hard to see that he'd finished the pint. He had his hat pushed way back on his head. The only time he did that was when he was sure enough drunk. He had wrapped his sore toe up in a pillowcase and there was sure as hell no boot on that foot. This made him walk a little short-legged but here he came just hollering and dancing a jig. I don't see how he could stand it on that sore foot, but it looked like he jumped higher on this one than the other. Me and Myrna quit dancing and so did everybody else. People on their way to the bathroom just clamped down and stopped to watch. Drinks were held an inch from the swaller hole without moving.

Wrangler ran right up to me and Myrna, circled about three times and then ran right under me and grabbed her.

"She looks just like Toy Smith, only better," he said. (Toy was a woman Wrangler had once had a big affair with.)

At first Myrna looked like she might booger and run, but when Old Wrangler threw his hat plumb across the bar and crowded up under that bosom and began to waltz her around slow and easy I knew we had something going. I slipped over to the bar and said to Dan (that was his name, Dan. I have always liked bartenders named Dan), "Dan," I said. "Dan, what's that woman do?"

He leaned over close and said, "Nothing."

That's all I wanted to know, because if she didn't do nothing she was either a whore or rich and I knew this one was rich. Wrangler would soon take care of the other part of that sentence.

Well, we all finally got settled back down at the table and Wrangler just moved in between Myrna and Gloria. He was talking low and fast. I didn't want to interrupt, but felt that now was the time to order a round of drinks on us. I could see that this crowd couldn't take many more. I was still being careful with our money.

Myrna said, "Martinis," to the waitress.

I'd never had one of them and I didn't figure Wrangler had, but I said, "All the way around."

When the waitress brought them old Wrangler acted as if he was going to pour it out. Then he said, "I ain't never had none of them before — none of them vegetables or nothing." And he whipped her up and polished it off with one and a half swallers.

We had another. This time Myrna bought. Now I kind

of appreciated that. Not only because we were being thrifty but because I never figured why a woman shouldn't buy a drink if she had the most money.

I liked that Myrna, but Wrangler liked her a hell of a lot more. That was fine with me, he was the one we were trying to marry off.

Myrna took out a mirror and sort of powdered her round, pretty face, patted at that short curly brown hair and stood up. Old Wrangler let out another yell and grabbed the silky-looking coyote hide. Myrna kind of jumped back.

Wrangler said, "I wasn't goin' to steal it or nothin'. I was just goin' to help you put it on."

That just about broke Myrna and the other girls up. The romance was on. They said they'd call us the next day and make a date for cocktails.

"By god," I said, "that's fine," and shook hands all around. We walked out to the car with them. It was a fancy-looking son of a bitch. I'd never seen one just like it before. It had RR wrote on it. Just the same I had already figured this was the kind she'd drive.

Wrangler told Myrna to bend over and he gave her one of those hungry kisses and I could see her wiggling in her lace pants. I couldn't make up my mind which one of the girls to tell goodnight, so I just kissed them all.

Nine

IT HAD TAKEN about an hour of knob-twisting before we could see that TV. It sure was loud, but I was afraid to turn anything again because nearly every time I touched one of those buttons the scene would change to a West Texas dust storm, or a long line of barbwire fence without any barbs.

A little feller was jumping up and down swallering a soda pop yelling "Drink Pep, it has the pepper to make you peppy!" Then a man dressed up something like a cowboy — I could tell he was faking it by the way he laid his saddle down on the skirts, no real cowboy would ever do that — took a long drag on a cigar. He was stretched out by a campfire and he gazed off at the moon just like he'd put his brand on ten head of his neighbor's calves. Then a coyote howled and another look came on his face. This time like a man who had just slept with his first woman. That feller had lots of different looks. I never figured it out for sure but I think he was really a cigar salesman.

Then a program started where a bunch of women got up and bawled and shed tears and a real kindhearted feller gave them iceboxes, electric stoves and such like. He sure was a generous man. It sorta surprised me. I thought they killed all that kind off.

After a while, a woman called Lolane was interviewed by a man dragging a bullwhip around. He talked with the handle right up next to his mouth. When Lolane talked he held it up next to hers. I don't rightly believe you can say she talked. She just sort of grunted the words and it seemed like she spoke with her chest instead of her mouth. I couldn't place it but something about her reminded me of Myrna.

We watched some of those westerns. I'm still confused about that. It seems that these fellers are called cowboys, but they spend most of their time in town drinking whiskey — which just goes to show that they are a heck of a lot smarter than most real cowboys. When they are out in the country, they never do any of the work cowboys do, they just lay behind rocks and blow people's heads off. It's pretty silly, but kinda fun to watch. This TV is an amazing invention.

The phone rang. We both jumped up and I said, "Answer it, Wrangler, that's Myrna."

"I don't talk over them damn thangs."

So I picked it up and tried to be *proper* as the town fellers say, and said "Hello" instead of "Howdy."

"Wrangler?" came oozing out over the phone so sweet

I could feel the silver melting off my belt buckle.

"No. This here's Dusty."

"Oh, hi, Dusty. Could I speak to Wrangler?"

"No."

A silence came over the phone and she finally said, "Well, why?" sort of short-like. I knew I had to make things right quick.

"Well, it's like this, Myrna. Wrangler's got one of them things about telephones. You know, what do you call it where a man's afraid of something without knowin' why?"

"A complex," she said.

"Yeah, that's it," I said, "he's got a boogery complex about telephones."

"Oh, how delightful," said Myrna. "Just tell the little darling that I'll be over to the Inn in about an hour."

"Are the girls coming, too?"

"No, they've gone shopping. Jane said to tell you she'd see you tomorrow."

I was a little let-down at first; then I really perked up. This was going to speed hell out of things, her coming over by herself. It sure looked good. Our luck was on the go.

She got there about three-thirty that afternoon. We were the only ones there. We had some more of those vegetable drinks and I gave that singing feller I'd liked so much the day before a dime every time he opened his mouth. It seemed like he knew a big romance was busting out. He really did do a good job, Myrna had already reached over and laid her left hand — the one with all them blue-white rings on it — under Wrangler's beat-up old fist and she was rubbing it like it was made of gold. Wrangler just went on drinking left-handed. I was just getting ready to leave them alone when a feller in a fine-looking speckled suit and a hat that didn't have hardly any brim at all came buttin' in. He was sucking on a pipe and rubbing a little bitty mustache. I could tell he was the vice-president of something or other. It seems to me that those vice-presidents all walk and talk alike.

"Hello, Myrna, darling," he spouted out like a big bird. "Where have you been, my dear? I've looked all over for you, precious. You look just divine, my pet. Simmmm-ppply divine!"

By god, I never heard anything like it. Less than thirty words and he had already called her darling, my dear, precious and divine. That man was a flattering fool. If he stayed an hour I wondered if he'd repeat himself.

I was surprised at how impolite the bastard was, considering his raising and all. He sat down at our table without even being introduced, much less asked. He just kept asking questions and answering them himself.

"I bet you've been to another of your flower shows. Of course you have, sweet. No, no. Let us see. Were you playing bridge at Esther's? That's it. I knew it, dumpling."

Myrna tried to say something but there just wasn't much use. I saw her pull her hand away from Wrangler's. I could tell she didn't want to.

On and on he rattled. New York and Hollywood, London and San Francisco kept coming up over and over.

Finally he kind of half covered his face with his hand and said, "Why, Myrna, you little rascal, leave it to you.

Wherever did you find these quaint gentlemen, my love?"

Myrna tried again. "Well, I . . ."

"Why on earth haven't you introduced us?" But before she could answer, the son of a bitch ordered *himself* a drink.

Well, I'll tell you this, I hated to spend the money, but I ordered three more vegetable drinks. This man, we finally found out that his name was Limestone Retch, kept right on blabbing.

"I wish the Monroes would improve their tennis court. They've talked about it for years. Louise is probably too busy in town, you know what I mean?" he said, looking sideways and flaring his nostrils like he'd just been told he was more of a dude than the Duke of Windsor. I could tell by that little "you know what I mean" business that somebody's throat was bleeding.

We had some more drinks. The sun was about to set. Some other people had come into the bar by now. The blabbing went on. He was getting a little drunk now and started telling dirty jokes. I heard every damn one of them when I was a kid. He was the only one who thought they were funny. He laughed so hard every time he finished telling one I kept hoping he'd bust something.

All of a sudden Wrangler said, "Do you swim, Limestone?"

"Wha . . . er . . . sure, but of course, all over the world, the finest places, Capri, Morocco, the Isle of . . ."

"Well, it's a damn good thing," old Wrangler said kind of humping up, "because I'm just fixin' to stir my drink with you."

Limestone swallered.

I swallered.

Myrna grinned sick-like.

I could see our ranch going to hell one way or the other right here. It was obvious that Limestone had just enough sense to understand that Wrangler was making headway with Myrna and it was just as obvious that Limestone had the same plan.

Wrangler was getting up on his sore foot, and I could tell he was going to do some damage to this vice-president's mustache.

I jumped up and ran around and said, "Come on, Limestone, I want to show you my horse. You ride, don't you, Limestone? Well, that's good. You'll like the looks of this ole pony. He's a dandy. Just wait till you see him." By god, it was my time to talk and I was doing it.

In the shank of the day I could still see Old Fooler's steel-muscled hind end sticking around the edge of the pickup. I let Limestone stumble out ahead of me and the damned fool walked around behind Old Fooler without speaking to him. Seems to me that as brilliant as this bastard's conversation was he'd have learned something in school. Damn near everybody knows you have to speak to a horse when you walk up behind him, otherwise he kicks. This is a throwback to the millions of years of time they spent being slipped up on by lions, tigers and such.

Blooey.

Whop.

Ooommmp.

Thud.

There wasn't much talking going on now. Limestone was stretched out there holding his belly and looking for some air. Old Fooler was jumping around, snorting and kicking right out over Limestone's head. But Limestone didn't know it. All he knew right then was that two cannon balls in the shape of horse's feet had whammed him in the belly.

I poured a half bucket of water on him that was too dirty for Old Fooler to drink and he kind of woke up. I just couldn't get that feller to talk to me. I tried and I tried. So, I thought to keep him from getting lonesome I ought to voice an opinion or two.

"Now, Limestone, you might think that hurt, but that's just like a loving mother rubbing powder on a week-old baby compared to what old Wrangler'll do to you. Leave Myrna alone. Do you hear me?"

He nodded and I could tell that the dumb bastard understood, so I helped him to his feet and he left, stumbling off without his pipe. He still wasn't saying anything. The quietened type I reckon.

I heard him drive off in one of those little peanut-looking cars. Then in a minute I could see Wrangler and Myrna heading for our room. I got my bedroll out of the pickup and told Old Fooler, "You have now been granted another week of life, you matchmakin' son of a bitch!"

Ten

THE SUN was up when I crawled out of my bedroll. I fed, and even brushed, Old Fooler down. This made him suspicious. He watched me close.

I said, "No, sir, Old Fooler, today we are friends. This here day will be celebrated sometime in the great future just like the Fourth of July, as the day the cowboys won. Whiskey'll run like spring rains, bands'll play and bribed judges and crooked lawyers will all make patriotic speeches."

I could tell Old Fooler didn't much believe me. Besides I decided I'd better shut up before I got to sounding like Limestone Retch.

I heard a noise so I looked around the edge of the pickup and saw Myrna leaving. She stepped off down to that big RR car like a madam with a full house. By god, I was nearly as happy as she was.

I dogtrotted over to the room. I just couldn't wait any longer.

By god, old Wrangler was learning fast. He was singing in the tub and soap was spilling out all over.

"Come in, Dusty, you no-good son of a bitch." That was the best thing Wrangler could say to a friend. I was happy.

I started to ask him how it went, then I saw the horrible condition of the bed and knew the deal was cinched.

"Did she get excited when you proposed to her, Wrangler?"

"She sure did. The poor thang fell out of bed!"

Things picked up from then on. Wrangler and Myrna went around everywhere together. She bought him a bunch of new tailor-made suits, shirts and boots. He even went so far as to wear a new hat when he was with her. They took in the opera, art shows, cocktail parties and such.

I made myself scarce during this period. Knowing they had plenty to do alone. In the meantime I had me three college girls to escort. The trouble was, for some reason, I liked this Miss Rollaway better than the others. The reason was hard to come by, because they were all pretty and paid their way.

I was learning fast just like Wrangler. I got to where I could operate one of those phones like a regular mechanic. I'd call her up and have her meet me somewhere without her friends. This helped to keep my spirits up while I waited for the great wedding to take place.

Finally Myrna had us all out to her house. It was out on the opposite side of town from the Ragoon Inn. She called it "the suburbs." Now the first thing I can say is that the house covered a whole lot of country. The rooms were all on different levels so it was hard to get from one to the other without falling down. This was impossible after a few of them vegetable drinks. It was one of those old Mexican adobe houses all smarted up with newfangled stuff — pictures, statues, pianos, bathrooms and bars. There were enough Navaho rugs on the floor to stock a curio store.

The outside was something to tell about, too. In the back yard was a big swimming pool all hemmed in with sandstone rocks. The same kind of sandstone I'd spent my whole life riding over and falling on, and here they'd found it useful. Paths wound around everywhere. Little fields of flowers were scattered all over. Myrna really loved those flowers. We were introduced to every plant on the place

"Look at my little darlings," she said, and reached out almost touching them. She talked to them like they were her kids.

All I could think of to say was, "Sure pretty."

Old Wrangler improved some on this. He said, "Mighty pretty."

I had heard she was an expert flower woman. I don't know if this meant she was an expert grower, smeller or raiser. It wouldn't have surprised me if she was good at all three.

We were sitting out by the swimming pool after our tour in the warm sun.

"Wrangler," I said, "when I was a kid all the poor folks lived on the edge of town; now it's the rich part."

"Everything changes," he said, firing up a cigar as long as a ruler and putting his brand-new kangaroo boots up on the table.

"Yeah, it sure does," I said, feeling happy at Wrangler's quick adjustment, but at the same time a little uneasy, too.

Myrna had the maid bring us a pitcher of drinks. I didn't know what they were and I damn sure wasn't going to ask. A man that would question free drinks ought to be hung in an outhouse like Wrangler said.

Myrna said, "Dusty, dear, would you like to bring your horse out here? We have the stables, you know? They're terribly empty. I just haven't had time to ride the last few years with the flowers and all to look after." She gazed out at all those short, tall, bunchy, skinny, red, yellow, white and purple flowers with the same look she had in her eyes for Wrangler. I knew the only competition he'd ever have would be those flowers.

"I sure would appreciate that, Myrna," I said. "It's some trouble over there at the Inn."

"You won't even have to worry about caring for him," she said. "I'll have the handy man do it."

Now by god ain't that a dinger. In a way I was already a foreman. Life sure enough looked good.

My main worry had been about Wrangler's conduct but like most of the things in the world I had strained my poor brains for nothing. In fact, if there was any worrying to do it was about him overdoing it.

One morning I saw him pick up a can of stuff and mash a button. Something sprewed out. He shot it under both arms, then sprayed some of it on his hair and combed it back slick and shiny. I slipped over directly and stole a look at the label. It was the same stuff they'd been advertising on TV: MASHO, FOR SMELLY MEN. PROTECTS ALL DAY. That's what it said on the can.

This might be all right for old society-climbing Wrangler but I'll be damned if I was ever going to admit I smelled that bad. But just the same he was doing better than all right. She was running by to pick him up in the RR car every little bit. And when she wasn't there the cockeyed phone was ringing. But the best sign of all was when she started handing him out a bunch of those brand-new fifty dollar bills. Then I knew old Wrangler had her as helpless as a tail-swinging monkey in a forest of sharp-spined cactus. That's to put it plain.

One day Wrangler came running in with a newspaper, yelling, "Look here! Look here! I got my name in the newspaper."

It said: "An engagement party will be held announcing the coming wedding of Miss Myrna Hopwell, Dime Store heiress (her third) to Mr. Wrangler Lewis (his first) of Hi Lo, New Mexico. Miss Hopwell lives on her estate near Ragoon, New Mexico, and is a specialist in mountain grown flowers. Mr. Lewis is engaged in the cattle and horse business."

"I never thought I'd see the time I'd get my name in the newspaper."

"Me neither," I said, but I was just about to bust a gut with pride. This here made it official. Nothing but a plague could keep me from being Wrangler's foreman now. I could just see the fat cattle and fine horses all over our ranch, and me riding around on the best horse in the country telling other people what to do. Oh, I'd be a decent son of a bitch about it. No dirty stuff like Jim Ed Love, but it would be a whole lot better boot to wear. I'll swear it looked like the improvements in this world would never end.

Eleven

THE ENGAGEMENT party brought on a pack of new experiences for me. I've never seen such a thing in my life.

At one end of the living room, on a flower-covered platform built for the occasion, was a four-piece band Myrna had — as she put it — "engaged." The other side of the room was nearly filled up with a twenty-foot long table running over with turkeys, hams and plate after plate of grub I never saw or heard of before. And besides a bowl of punch as big as a horse trough, she had two bartenders behind the bar working themselves plumb rattle-headed trying to empty all those whiskey bottles. They did a good job, but it took them all night.

Yes sir, this was sure as hell going to be a party of engagements all right.

People were as crowded as fingers on a closed fist and more kept coming in. Myrna had Wrangler by the arm introducing him to all the people around the room.

All these new faces made me nervous. I was really wishing Miss Rollaway and her friends could have made it home from school for this blowout. I finally eased my way over and told the bartender to fill my glass.

"Soda water?" he asked.

"No, whiskey," I said. I turned that old glass up and drank'r so empty it looked like a brand-new one.

"Again?"

"Again!"

It wasn't a very big glass but I felt more sociable and I had learned why they sometimes called these get-to-gethers cocktail parties.

A feller walked up to me and said, "How do you do, old chap? I hear from Myrna you are in actuality a real, working cowboy."

I didn't want to get into any more discussions trying to tell this Englishman I was an ex-cowboy, so I just said, "That is right."

"Well, it is my pleasure to introduce myself. I am Sir Shambles, Ambassador at Large for Her Majesty. I'm now stationed in the Islands. I flew over for Myrna's party. Good girl. Old friends, you know?"

I didn't know, but I nodded my head and took a sip of whiskey.

"When I heard she was marrying one of the cow people I could hardly contain my interest. You see we English pioneered the cattle industry in America."

This here did sort of set me back on my hunkers. I'd never really thought about how it started. It seemed like to me it had always been here, long as I could remember, at least.

"Is that right?" I said.

"Indeed, it is, my dear fellow. The old XIT Ranch in the Texas Panhandle is only one of the rather large estates instigated by English capital."

I took a liking to this feller right then and there, but before I could get some real friendly talk going a herd of fat old women ran off with him, just introducing one another so fast I thought they were going to tear the poor feller in half.

I learned something else I didn't know — just get you a drink and stand in one place. All kinds of folks will come up and talk to you. If you move about it becomes *your* responsibility to start the talk.

This feller walked up to me and said, "I'm Jack Garfield."

"I'm Dusty Jones."

"I'm vice-president of . . ."

I knew it, by god, I knew it. Another one of them. I started to bust him right off and then I remembered I was on good behavior till after the wedding.

"I was just over at Judge Malhead's yesterday. Know him? Fine man. Great person. We're just like this. He said to me, 'Jack,' he said, 'we've been friends a long time haven't we?' 'Yes, we have, Judge.' 'Well,' he said, 'I'm going to let you in on a big thing. Something *really* big. Get me? You have to swear by the utmost secrecy not to let this out.' I looked the judge straight in the eye and said, 'Judge, you know me better than that.' 'All right, Jack,' he said, 'here it is. They're going to build a new electronic plant here in Ragoon. It's going to be put on the Smith property.' Well, I'll have you know, Mr. Jones, that *I* just

this morning closed a deal for all the surrounding property for *our* company. How do you like that? Fast work,
eh?"

"Well, I'll be a goddamned chicken-stealing, lamb-killing coyote," I said.

This seemed to please him because he said, "Mr. Jones,
if you ever need anything, any little favors, just let me
know. I can get to the judge anytime. Of course there are
certain little favors one has to give in return. Convention,
you know. Just business. Plain business."

For a minute there he had me thinking he really meant
it. But when he got to that "certain favors" part I knew
I was out.

He was starting out on another one of his smart deals
when this fat woman came up and started talking to
him.

I slipped over sideways but before I could take another
drink one of those fat women grabbed me. Her eyes
bugged out like two tiny burned-out light bulbs. She was
wearing so many necklaces they pulled her forward. I
had the notion to give her a push and get her straightened
up.

"My darling" (by god the world was full of darlings).
"I'm so glad for Myrna. She's really been lonely these last
years. Of course, she has her flowers and uh, of course, all
those millions to comfort her. And uh, you will be good
to her won't you, darling?"

"Yeah," I said.

"She needs someone she can trust, you know? And uh,
someone to lean on in time of tribulation. Of course, we

all do," she said and kind of shook like something was binding her.

"I ain't the one," I said.

"Whatever do you mean?" she said, and gave me a look that would have scared a natural born coward flat to death.

"I mean, I ain't marrying Myrna."

"Well!" she said and hustled off twisting all over trying to get out of that bind.

I decided it was time I changed locations. I went to the bar. Then I squatted down behind a little tree planted in a great big bowl. Three or four people were talking at once. Finally one of them got louder than the others.

"I tell you the evils of the world are rooted in organizations: communism, religion, marriage and yes, even capitalism."

"Capitalism an organization?" somebody said.

"Exactly. You know we all know. We're afraid to admit it. Look at all the organized good we've done to all the primitives in the world. They were happy until the capitalist and the communist started showing them the difference. Death, pain, love and beauty were all accepted for what they are — simply part of the universe. But now we've ruined them. We've educated them. Ha!" He was getting louder all the time. "The only truth, the only government worthwhile has been found in a monarchy."

Since I didn't savvy a thing they were talking about I got up and made another move. Across the room, poor old Wrangler was still going strong on that handshaking.

Marrying a rich woman wasn't quite as simple as I thought.

I saw a lonesome-looking feller sitting on a window seat. I ambled over and said, "Howdy."

He looked up at me out of sneaky, sad eyes, rubbed his beard and nodded.

"Nice party, ain't it?" I said.

"It will do, I suppose."

"You live around here?" I asked, trying to get something going.

"Oh, temporarily. New York is my home. I'm just here on, well, shall we say research."

He waited like he wanted me to ask him what kind of research. But I didn't.

So he said, "I'm a poet."

Well I'll be damned if he didn't look and act just like I thought a poet would. Course I don't know any poets.

There was a commotion outside around the swimming pool. People had started pushing one another into the water with all their clothes on. They had to get pretty drunk to do it, but it was happening just the same. They were laughing real loud like this was the funniest thing in the world. I was getting a little worried about my sense of humor. Maybe I was losing it.

I turned back to the poet and said, "Come on, let's grab us a girl and dance and holler and have some fun."

He looked at me another minute and said like it was making him sick, "You call *that* fun?"

Well before I could grab me a girl, a great big husky man with a bowtie on walked up and said, "There's no use. They are just no good."

"Huh?" I said.

"Thass right. They are *no damn good.* She's gone to her aunt's. Sheesh taken the kids. My kids," he said, and started crying and rubbing his round face.

"Who?" I asked.

"My wife. She won't be my wife any longer. I just can't understand it. When we first got married we were so happy. I didn't get to stay home much. The business was just starting. Had to make a go of that. A man's got to make a go of that, hasn't he?"

"I reckon he has," I said.

"Well, he does. You just can't get along unless you make a go. You're left out. I worked sixteen hours a day making it go. It went," he said, sniffing and looking up at the ceiling. "Yeah, it went. I just don't understand it. I gave her everything. Clothes, cars, one of the best homes in town. She had a maid. We made all the clubs in town. Look," he said, and pulled out a billfold that unfolded like an accordion. "Look. You see these?"

"Unhuh. What are they?"

"What are they? Credit cards, that's what they are. Look. I have five different gasoline cards. Three diners, two . . . one . . ." and he just kept rattling "This is my country club card and I belong to the Masons, Kiwanis and Lions. Now, if that isn't proof, where is it?"

When he said "proof" I thought maybe he was in some kind of trouble with the law. But that wasn't it at all. It was his wife he was trying to prove something or other about.

All that whiskey I'd drunk made me feel helpful, so I said, "You have to make love to 'em ever' day."

"Every day?"

"Ever' day."

"I don't have time for that."

It was my turn to talk so I said, "And that ain't all you've got to do. You've either got to beat hell out of them or make 'em ragin' mad about something at least once a week."

"You do? Why?"

"I don't know why and I don't care why, but that's the only way they love you."

"Oh! Oh, I couldn't do that," he said, "she'd sue me. Why she'd take everything *I* own!"

I wasn't doing this feller much good so I just walked off looking for someone else to help. It didn't take long. This little woman, or girl I reckon you'd call her, just latched onto me and turned the most pitiful set of eyes up to me I nearly ever saw. She looked kinda like a kitten that had just been spanked by a mouse.

"He's done it again," she said.

"Lord a mercy, what?"

"Got himself tied up for another five years. Says he'll be president of the company in another five years."

"What is he now?"

"He's vice-president now. First vice-president."

"There you go," I said.

"There you go where?"

"Oh, nothing."

"Well, I told him that I'd like to hear something just once besides business and promotions. Just once. And another thing I didn't tell him about is all those silly dinners he makes me go to. I'm supposed to smile at some numbhead all evening and listen about his conquests of the business world. Of his clever little subtilities to get and keep the advantage over his cohorts."

"His what?"

"His associates."

"Let's go get us a drink," I said.

She patted her smooth hair and said, kind of surprised, "Well, all right."

I no longer had to tell the bartender how I wanted my drinks. And I said, "The lady will take one just like it."

She said, "How do you know I'll like it?"

I said, "I don't, but if you're goin' to drink with me that's what you'll drink."

She smiled, "I'm game."

We had another drink. I don't hardly think she was used to this kind of cocktail hour, so I just eased her around and danced with her.

She said, "My, that was nice."

"It sure was."

Then she started blabbing again. "It's to the point now that we're sleeping in separate bedrooms."

I said, "I just can't believe it. Why I never heard of such a silly thing."

"It is true," she said, and tears started running down on her pretty little cheeks.

Here was somebody I could help. I led her around through all those drinking, talking, arm-waving people and down aways to a dark room. I couldn't find a bed in it but it didn't hold things up much. I just grabbed her and kissed her and threw her down on the rug. All she ever got to say was "No . . . noooo."

It wasn't long till this woman was feeling a whole lot better. I even felt some better myself.

She told me, "Thanks."

And I said, "Glad to do it."

I let her go back to the crowd first, then in a bit I followed.

Everybody was looking over towards a sure-enough fancy woman. I'll be a chicken-stealing, lamb-killing coyote if it wasn't that Lolane I'd seen on TV the other day.

Myrna was introducing old Wrangler to her. In a minute he threw his head up and looked around until he spotted me. He waved one of his short, heavy arms for me to come over. I went.

That Lolane's hair was so blond her shadow looked bleached, but everything else seemed real. Real good, in fact. Everything except the feller that was with her. He was about a foot taller than me. His hair was slick and black and so shiny in places it looked like he had deep barbwire cuts in his head. He just smiled and smiled and smiled.

"Hello there," he said to everybody he met, and he flashed that row of white teeth till I thought he was going to split a lip.

Well, sir, the next thing I knew I was dancing with Lolane. It was a real pleasurable thing to do. She was a little silly at first saying such things as . . . "My, it's hot in here, isn't it? I just think Myrna's house is too too. I'm starting a new picture next week. It has the most divine cast, and the script is just too too. I'm tired of it though. Some day I'm going to settle down in a little place like Ragoon and just do nothing but read."

This last kind of made me taste the steel bits in my mouth. There were so many things a woman like this could do to have fun besides read. Damn near anybody could read. Even old Wrangler knew almost half the words in the Ragoon newspaper.

Poor girl. Everybody stared at her except her husband; he was over talking to the poet. They were flinging fingers at one another in what looked to me like an insulting manner. Course you couldn't tell about that cause one of them smiled all the time and the other one never did.

When the music stopped, everybody gathered around us. They kept wanting to meet her or say something to her or in some way be recognized.

"By god," I said right in the middle of the next dance, "come out here. I want to show you my horse." I'd heard about these artists and fancy folks showing their etchings. Well, I show my horse.

"Reckon your husband'll miss us?"

"Oh, he's not my husband. Why I haven't been married in weeks. Ray's gay. It just looks good for us to be seen together."

"Yeah," I said, "he does seem kind of gay. Smiles all the time."

"You're kidding," she said.

I couldn't figure how she figured I was kidding so I just dropped that subject.

She held tight to my arm and snuggled up a little as we walked down the path to the stables. Now I'm not one to carry on much about scenery, but man, what a night.

Old Fooler was standing near the middle of the corral in the bright moonlight with his head down and he didn't bother to look up.

"There he is," I said.

"Is he a good one?" she asked. "Is he spirited?"

"Yes, Miss Lolane, you are looking at one of the most spirited animals on earth."

"Oh, that's just too too," she said, and kind of shook all over. "I made a western," she said. "Did you see it?"

"No, I don't reckon so. What was it called?"

"*We Fit,*" she said. "It flopped."

A coyote howled off in the hills behind the stable. "My goodness," she said and crowded up closer. "He sounds like he's crying so so sad."

"No, ma'am, that animal's laughing."

"Laughing?"

"*That* is right."

"Well, what on earth does the poor thing have to laugh at?"

"Why, he's laughin' at us people."

"Why would he do that?"

"He's smarter, that's why."

"You're kidding," she said.

Now I was beginning to like Lolane, but I could see right now I was going to have to get her over the idea I was always kidding. So, I took her in the corral to get a closer look at my spirited horse. Then I showed her my saddle where the moonlight shot through the stable door. Then I threw the saddle blanket down in that pale blue shaft of moonlight.

She said, "What did you do that for?"

Bless that old coyote's laughing heart, he howled again before I could answer. She made another one of those shaky snuggles and I gathered her up right against my levi buttons.

She made out like she was going to pull away, but I could feel her hoping I wouldn't let her. I didn't. I took hold of that little pouty red mouth with mine. She wanted this. I felt up and down her back until my hand found that dress zipper, then smooth as silk I slid it down.

Stars above! When I stepped back, that low-hung dress just dropped off on the ground. That dress had been her entire wardrobe. We dropped right down beside it onto the saddle blanket. Now I knew why she reminded me of Myrna. They were so big it took both hands to give one of them a good feel. But no problems, I have two hands.

"Ohhhh," she said, and by doggies we made love.

At first she acted a little like she was in the habit of doing it just to be nice, but in a minute more she was loving because she liked it.

It was a beautiful, soft, warm place so we lay awhile longer and let the goodness soak all through us.

After a little, she put her mouth to my ear and whispered, "That horse is watching us."

I looked around and sure enough there Old Fooler stood with his ears pitched forward. I whispered back, "It's all right, he won't tell anybody."

All of a sudden, I jumped up, grabbed her by the hands and pulled her to her feet. Then I just turned her around in that beam of moonlight and looked. She was a hell of a lot prettier than her pictures.

I walked around and took a look at her rear. It was about the prettiest thing I'd ever seen. Old Wrangler is a milk-cow man. He likes big-chested women. Well they're just fine, but I'm more of a quarter-horse man myself. It's those hindquarters that set me to going.

Then I circled her while she trembled and shivered all over. She was breathing so hard I got worried and thought I better get her bedded down again.

It was better than before. By god if this woman had been out of the spotlight awhile and had the right training she'd have been the champion lover of the whole United States.

We rested again.

Then she said, "Darling, hand me my dress." When I did, she kind of straightened it out and started trying to put it on while still sitting down. She did it!

I said, "I'll be a goddamned chicken-stealing, lamb-killing coyote!"

She said, "Nothing to it. Experience in the dressing room."

Just like I figured, all she needed was experience.

We got up and told Old Fooler goodnight. I could have sworn he had an evil grin on his face. She walked along holding my arm, her head kind of over on my shoulder. She said, "That was nice. It was real."

I didn't say anything.

The next thing we heard was old Wrangler taking on

out in the patio. I kind of hurried up, getting a little scared. Here we were just a half mile from heaven and I didn't want anything to happen.

A crowd was gathered around the pool. Almost everybody had already either jumped in or been thrown in. I reckon this foolishness is what gave Wrangler the idea. He was standing at the edge of the pool with Myrna hanging on to his arm. She looked a little drunk, so I don't think she was being loving or comforting at the moment, but mainly trying to stand up.

The Englishman was standing close by with a big wad of money in each hand taking bets. "Now," he said, "since my countrymen were the pioneers, yea, the very creators of these cow people, and since Mr. Wrangler Lewis is one of that fast-vanishing breed, I will say with all sincerity and implicit faith, I believe he can do what he says! Step right up and place your bets!"

Everybody was looking for gambling money. The vice-president was trying to make a bet on the strength of his credit cards.

All of a sudden Wrangler downed a big vegetable drink, threw the glass up in the air and started singing:

Jesus loves me this I know
For the Bible tells me so.
He will wash me white as snow
Dirty, dirty job for Jesus.

Yes sir, this society bunch had given Wrangler religion.

I grabbed the Englishman's shoulder and asked, "What's he goin' to do? What're you all bettin' on?"

He looked at me and said, "My dear fellow, your

pardner maintains he is going to walk across the pool."

"My god, he thinks he's Jesus!" I yelled, and tried to get through the crowd to stop him. I was too late. He had bent down and picked up one of those loose sandstone rocks right out of the patio floor. Then he walked to the edge of the pool and stepped off. What with holding that big rock and the fact he couldn't swim, he went right to the bottom. And in the deepest part too!

The crowd was quiet.

Myrna screamed, "Save my love!"

I grabbed her and said, "Look!" For there in that pale green water stepped old Wrangler. He walked clean across the bottom of that pool, and when he got to the shallow end his head came out like a turtle's. He was blowing to beat hell. But who wouldn't be, he'd been walking uphill.

The deed was so full of courage that nobody argued any technical points. Instead they hauled him out of the water and a great shout rose from their drunken throats.

Myrna cried, "My hero!"

The Englishman gave Wrangler half the winnings and I just walked over and patted Lolane on her beautiful butt.

It couldn't have been a finer world.

Twelve

ON THIS PARTICULAR morning, we got up by inches.

I said, "All the time I thought I'd been pourin' them drinks in my stomach, they'd been goin' in my head."

"I feel like I've been pulled through a half-inch water pipe a mile long," Wrangler answered, sitting up trying to get the hair out of his eyes. "Anything to drink around here?"

"Nothing but about an inch and a half of stale wine in that bottle over there," I said, pointing to a dresser.

He got up, weaved over and stared at the bottle. "I'd rather drink carbolic acid than that stuff," he said, and picked up the bottle and drained her dry with one swaller. I thought he had a funny-looking face till now. But the one he made after that wine was just too damn bad for even his best friend to look at.

I got up, put on my pants and boots and stumbled down to the coke machine. I felt bad. I had enough of this drinking to do me for nine years. Maybe forever.

I put a dime in the machine and got my coke. When I got back to our door I said, "Wrangler, want a coke?"

"Hell no, what time is it?"

I looked at the sun, "Oh, about eight-thirty."

"The bar opens in thirty minutes," he said.

"You ain't goin' to drink again today, are ya'?" I said. "Hell, the wedding's tomorrow."

"Well," he said, making good sense, "we've been celebratin' the engagement for nine days now, we ought to toast the weddin' itself for at least one."

I couldn't argue. The best thing I could do was see that he didn't get too drunk. Now that was going to be a grind.

We started out by having a couple of beers in the Inn. Then we ordered three eggs and a big chunk of ham with some black coffee. The world began to look a little bit like it had the day before.

I knew Myrna was busy getting ready for the wedding, and if she wanted Wrangler she'd look for him at the Inn. I didn't want to take a chance on anything happening so I said, "Come on, let's hunt another bar. This'n here is tired of us."

"Whatever suits you just tickles me plumb to death," he said, being agreeable as long as I was looking for a bar.

Well, by ten o'clock that morning we had found one a lot closer in town. It was dirty and dark and run by a Mexican. I figured old Wrangler would kinda like this. It's the only kind of joint he's used to. But he wouldn't say much when I talked. Maybe this high living was spoiling him.

"Well, tomorrow it'll all be over," I said, feeling better by the minute. "You'll have a good-looking rich woman. One you can truly love. That's cake with icing, boy. In a few days we'll buy that nice cow outfit and I can go to work running it for you. I bet you never thought that would happen to us, did you, pardner?"

At the word "pardner" he threw his head up, grunted and motioned to the bartender to bring us another round.

"Tell you what we better do, Wrangler. Soon as we get our ranch tied up, we better start building us a rodeo arena. On Sunday afternoons we can invite the local boys over for calf roping and maybe a little wild-cow milking and bronc riding."

"Had all the bronc riding I want." He was staring at a Mexican gal that must have been the sister of the bartender.

I saw she was fairly good looking. I thought I'd better really move in fast. Old Wrangler might just blow everything. I played the music and asked her to dance.

She stood a minute, looked at the bartender, shrugged her shoulders and said, "Why not?"

We danced and we danced. Then I'd set her down at the bar and we'd have another drink. I didn't let her out of reach. I could read that look on Wrangler's bulldog face too damn well.

Then I saw him heading for us. It was too late, he'd already set his mind on dancing with this little gal. I can't say as I blamed him. I reckon he figured this would be one last fling before he married. On the other hand he might not be thinking any such thing. He might just like her because she was a girl.

I thought fast. "Wrangler," I said, and it was the truth, "Myrna told me to be sure that you got a blood test today. She said it would ease her mind about the Rh Factor."

He stopped, blinking his little snake eyes, he said, "What's that?"

"Well, I don't exactly know, but she said it ran in her family, and it has something to do with having kids."

I'll be damned if it didn't work. He went back to the table and just stared.

A great big noise boomed outdoors. I jumped about three yards.

The bartender said, "It's raining."

It sure was. I could hear that water just splashing all over.

"Wrangler," I said, "you better take the pickup and run on in and see Dr. Price. That's who Myrna said was to give you the blood test."

"It's raining," he said, and just went on staring at a place on the side of the bar.

Finally I could see that Wrangler was afraid to go to the doctor so I walked up to a ragged-looking toothless old boy who was drinking the cheapest wine in the house. I asked him a question.

"Do you know where Dr. Price's office is?"

"Sure," he said. "I ain't never met him but the old lady goes there all the time fer her rheumatiz."

After a little explaining, two more drinks and a ten-dollar bill, he agreed to go to this Dr. Price and tell him his name was Wrangler Lewis and get a blood test.

Anything to please the new wife of my new boss.

I went back up and had another drink with the girl. Just in case his mind swung around to her again. Several people came in and all except one said, "It's raining." This one feller (he was about as big as me and Wrangler put together) came in, his arm swung around the shoulder of a half-pregnant woman. I'm sure they'd been celebrating something or other, for he said, "Who's raining?"

He had on a brand-new green shirt and she wore a loose flopping red dress. Where the rain had dropped off the shirt onto her dress there were green stripes. By god, she looked like a battle flag. They ordered muscatel wine, a sure sign of their condition whether they were drunk or not.

Wrangler was still staring at the bar, but this woman had filled up the spot he was hypnotized by. Pretty soon this big bastard with the big ears and big mouth noticed Wrangler staring. He walked over and said, "Hey, quit lookin' at my woman!"

Wrangler didn't even look up.

"I said, quit looking at my woman!" and he leaned over with his fists spread out on the table.

"What woman?" Wrangler asked.

"That'n," he said, pointing at the big-bellied red dress with the green stripes over the shoulders.

"I ain't staring at her," Wrangler said, scooting his chair around.

Now it makes no difference where you go in the world

there will always be one of these smart bastards to ruin a man's fun. But he might upset a lot more than that if he happened to land that wad of bone he used for a hand in the middle of Wrangler's face. We might have to postpone the wedding.

I got up, walked over and said, "Wrangler, this man is a head taller than you are, so I'm goin' to even things up."

I grabbed the son of a bitch around the neck and tried to pull his head off. It wouldn't come. I took another run across the room with him. I could see Wrangler was trying to help. He was pulling in the other direction. But one of the old boy's shoes came off and Wrangler fell backwards. Without this added weight we really began to move. The only thing that stopped us was a cement wall. I couldn't pull his head off and I couldn't drive it through the wall, so I just dropped him there and yelled, "Let's go."

On the way out, I could see the bartender calling the cops on the phone and I asked him, "Why didn't you stop that bastard from picking on my little friend? Then you wouldn't have to call the cops."

I didn't hear what he said because we stepped out into the rain. Our tough-necked friend failed to follow.

We jumped in the pickup, and I want to say that my lightning brains were still working. "Now, where will the police expect a couple of half-drunk cowboys to head?"

"Out of town," Wrangler said.

"*That* is right, so *up* town we're goin'!"

Thirteen

WE MANAGED to get uptown without having a wreck.

I even got the pickup parked fairly close to the curb. Wrangler wanted to head for another bar. I figured I ought to try to delay this.

"Listen, Wrangler, do you realize you ain't even bought Myrna a wedding present?"

"Never thought of it."

"Well now's the time. Come on, let's look around town here and see what we can find."

The rain had stopped and everybody was out on the sidewalk looking around. First we went in a store called a Five and Dime. I'll say this though, that sign was a big lie. The only thing in there for five cents was a package of chewing gum. We walked around looking at all those things: Bottles of everything on earth, hairpins, hairnets, hair spray, face powder, hand powder, and powder for other places, shoes, dishes, drawers for both men and girls.

They were pink, blue, yellow, red and all the colors in Myrna's flower garden. This brought something to mind.

"Wrangler, what does Myrna love more than anything on earth besides you?"

He kind of twisted his face around and said, "Them vegetable drinks." He acted so dang pleased with this that I hated to disappoint him.

"No, you're wrong. It's flowers."

"You're right," he said, getting the idea.

We walked over and bought a large, dun-colored flower-pot with a little baby lemon tree in it. They wrapped it all up and told Wrangler to be careful with it.

"I will," he said.

We barely left the store when he spotted another sa-loon. I knew I couldn't stop him from going in but maybe I could talk him into leaving soon. Seems like he was more shook up than ever before.

He downed three double shots while I coasted along on two singles. That brain of mine, that was getting so light-ning fast lately, started working again.

"You know, Wrangler, Myrna is goin' to ask us the first thing in the morning how we spent our day. Now wouldn't it be nice if we could say we spent it at the mov-ing pictures."

"All right that's what we'll tell her," he said motioning for another double shot.

"It ain't quite that easy." I said. "What if she asks what we saw?"

"That ain't no problem," he said, "the picture show's right around the corner."

"You ain't gettin' what I mean. What if she has seen this show herself and starts pumping us about it?"

"Oh."

"Drink up and let's go."

He gathered up his flowerpot easy-like and we walked around to the show. It had a big sign out front:

THE IRON SPIDER

A MONSTER DROPPED FROM OUTER SPACE TO

DEVOUR THE WORLD

I bought us a couple of tickets and we went in. They had a little old place that looked like a bar where they sold chewing gum, candy, soda pop and popcorn. I ordered us a bag of popcorn apiece, but when I handed it to Wrangler he said, "That ain't enough. I'm hungry." So he ordered two more bags.

I said, "How're you goin' to handle three bags of popcorn and that lemon tree?"

He didn't answer. He just took off his hat and emptied all the popcorn in it. We went to the show.

It was hard to see in there and we both had the blind staggers. A little feller carrying a flashlight without any light in it, took us down in the middle of the place and we finally got settled.

The show was just starting. A great big flat-looking thing was flying over the top of the world. Inside it was a bunch of green men who had a face in front and the same face in back. Their feet were the same way. They reminded me of some of those little peanut cars you see around these big towns. I watched and I watched but there wasn't any way to tell the front from the back. I kept thinking that maybe if one of their women would show up a feller might get a clue.

All of a sudden a lot of loud, scary music started playing (I never did see where the band was but it played during the whole show) and a great big iron spider dropped out of that flying machine. It came down on a thread like any spider would except it was about seven jillion times bigger. On the ends of its iron legs were some bucket-looking things. Soon as it landed it started sticking out those iron legs and sucking everything right up into that big belly. It was sure enough boogery.

Then the scene changed to a wad of scientific fellers talking to the army, and one of the army fellers wasn't no feller at all, it was a woman who looked a little like Lolane. They were calling out army tanks, and thousands of soldiers and airplanes by the hundred. But this spider just went right on through this city knocking over buildings as big as mountains, swatting airplanes out of the sky like sick mosquitoes, and sucking people up those iron legs as fast as he got to them. One of those science fellers said that human food was like fuel to this monster. He really had plenty, looked like to me.

Wrangler was chewing popcorn so hard and fast that folks all around were turning to us and saying, "Shhhhh." They gave us dirty looks too.

After a while that spider took in after a handsome soldier and this pretty woman. He stuck out one of those iron legs and slowly but surely that poor woman was pulled right up into that bucket.

It was too much for Wrangler. He jumped up and yelled, "Kill the mean son of a bitch!" Popcorn went everywhere. People got all upset, and the little man with the flashlight came down and told us to be quiet or leave. I finally got Wrangler settled enough to watch the picture.

The woman was completely gone and the soldier was fighting like hell trying to hang on to the edge of the iron leg. Then all of a sudden the spider sort of fell backwards trembling and began to weave and sink lower and lower. Finally he fell over, kicked a time or two and died. It sure was a relief.

I was really surprised at how smart that soldier was. Come to find out that wasn't a real woman at all — just a dummy made of wax. The wax choked that spider to death and thereby the world was saved.

Wrangler just sat there pumping his lungs after the show was over.

We finally got enough strength to get outside. I expected it to be dark but the sun was still two hours high. Wrangler didn't say a word. He was shaking all over and his eyes were kind of glazed like melted glass. He could see good enough though to read a sign that said HARRY'S SALOON.

He commenced pouring those drinks down and the most I could get out of him was his usual grunt. This didn't look good. The more he drank the more I could tell that spider was on his mind. I played the jukebox, and told all sorts of lies trying to get his mind off the show. Nothing worked.

After a while I said, "Let's go to another saloon."

He got up and followed me out. We walked down the street without talking. I was hoping I could get him to the pickup and haul him back to the Inn. Then I figured I'd get him in the room with a full bottle and just let him forget all these things that seemed to be on his back.

Well we passed a doorway and on the window next to it was a sign that said:

BETTY'S BEAUTY
SALON

Now Wrangler's not very tall when he's stepping his highest, and I reckon the only word he saw was the bottom one. He just automatically turned in. I followed.

There sat eight ladies under eight hair dryers. Some were cleaning their fingernails, others were reading.

Old Wrangler stiffened like a frozen post. Then he hauled off and threw his flowerpot at one of the hair dryers. His aim was good. The dryer banged, the pot broke and the dirt and the lemon tree all came down on top of the woman's fresh-washed head.

Then with a wild yell he attacked one of the dryers. The women jumped all directions, overturning things. The ones who didn't faint ran out in the street screaming "Police! Police! Madman!"

Wrangler didn't seem to notice anything like this. He had one of the hair dryers down choking hell out of it and when that didn't seem to make any difference he began to beat it against the floor.

He was yelling, "Don't worry ladies, I'll kill this god-damned iron spider!"

Well, he killed several before the police got there. I just stood and watched. I'd already given up. It was just too much for old tired Dusty.

The police grabbed him and I said, "Here now, this man's a hero. He's drunk and he thought those dryers were spider legs."

With that they just loaded me up and took me along with the hero. Right in jail they threw us and locked the thick iron door. Now an old uncle of mine (the one that wasn't a preacher) once told me that if you were on a party and didn't get in jail, you hadn't had any fun. This was one time he was wrong. What really got me was that before I could chew Wrangler's tail out, the little ugly bastard had gone to sleep.

There ain't no use whatever in telling all about the night. It was long.

The next morning after one of those sorry jail breakfasts, we went before the judge. I tried like hell to remember the vice-president's name who'd offered his help at Myrna's party. I just couldn't think straight all of a sudden. Then I thought about calling Myrna and realized that my lightning brain was slipping a little there, too. If she didn't find out about this we'd have old Wrangler hitched today and then it would be too late. Yes, sir, today was the day.

Well, the judge let us know right off that he was God and owned the world and could do anything he wanted to with us. I agreed with everything he said. I'd learned long ago that there's no justice with judges. Especially if you talk back.

He then proceeded to fine us the limit, for drunkenness, disturbing the peace, fighting and destroying several inanimate objects. Namely hair dryers. Then on top of that we had to pay for those hair dryers. Our rate of payment was based on the price of brand-new ones, even though they were several years old. We paid. The price for being a hero really comes high these days.

I was glad to get out of there even though we only had six dollars and eighty-four cents left out of all our pay, all Myrna's fifty-dollar bills and all that money the Englishman had given us. It was a damn good thing it was the day of the great wedding.

Fourteen

I'LL SAY one thing, *that* Myrna doesn't do *any*thing half-way. People were driving up in Cadillacs and RR cars from just about everywhere.

Out by the swimming pool three cooks wearing great tall white hats were barbecuing a whole beef. They kept turning him over the coals and on a windy day you could have smelled it as far as Hi Lo. It made a feller's taster act up. Four or five waiters were running around with their hands turned upside down carrying trays of vegetable drinks.

It was sunshiny and the wind was still. People were seated all around the swimming pool, talking and drinking and waiting. Every little bit a car would drive up and unload an armload of flowers. It made me kind of sad that our lemon tree hadn't survived the picture show.

Old Fooler was standing with his head up over the corral looking wild-eyed. He was getting fat and mean.

Myrna called me into the house to try to help Wrangler get ready. It sure was a job mashing him into that tuxedo. In fact, we never did get him in it completely.

The phone kept ringing and Myrna would answer, "Oh, I'm so sorry you couldn't make it, dear. Well, thank you, dear. How are things in New York? Tell Joe 'Hello' for me, darling. Oh yes, he's a sweetie pie. We'll be so happy. Yes, dear, we'll see you in Mexico in January. I will. I will. Bye now."

It just kept on — one thing after another. Then the preacher came in and made a big show out of what was going to take place. It seems we missed some kind of rehearsal.

Myrna's personal maid loped in with the daily paper all spread out and her finger pointing to a certain spot on the front page. I got the cold feeling a baby mouse must get when he's just been swallered by a rattlesnake.

Myrna said, "Not now, Celia, I can't read now. What is it that's so important?"

I made several signs at the maid but she smiled back exactly like Old Fooler after he's kicked you in the belly.

"Madam," she said, "it's *very* important."

Myrna stopped what she was doing and said, "All right, I don't suppose a minute longer will hurt, will it, honey pie?"

Old Wrangler grinned back kind of silly-like, "I reckon not, Myrna baby."

I had already read over her shoulder all I wanted to see and that was this:

Heiress' Bridegroom Spends Pre-Wedding Night in Jail

Myrna turned white even through that suntanned makeup. She glared at Wrangler and spit out, "The cinema my foot!"

Before Myrna could say more, the maid handed her the phone, halfway shouting with excitement, "It's Dr. Price. He says its extremely urgent."

Myrna took the phone. She was shaking so hard it rattled against her golden earrings.

"What? An alcoholic? And it showed positive on . . . on . . . !" and right there words failed her. Whatever was positive must've really been bad. She dropped the phone right across Wrangler's head, screaming, "You filthy beast, you've given me that horrible disease." Then she threw the mirror, and a big bottle of lotion. She tried to throw the dressing table. Then she just stopped and screamed and pulled her hair. "You beast, you vile beast!"

I gathered up the little beast's boots, levis and his shirt. He grabbed his hat and we retreated. I will say this, Myrna's screams had only interested the guests. I heard one of them say as we broke out of the house, "Seems the groom is taking advantage of his marriage privileges somewhat early." But when they saw the groom barefooted with a big, old, greasy cowboy hat on and his little potbelly hanging out over those shiny black britches, a lot of voices stilled, but not Myrna's. We could still hear her screaming.

"Listen," I said, thinking lightning fast, "she'll calm down in a minute and you'll just have to tell her the truth. That we sent somebody else in your place. That wasn't *your* POSITIVE blood at all."

Wrangler just stood there shaking. He had a ten-day hangover to help him, but I believe his courage would have snapped anyway.

She was at an open window now still pulling her hair and yelling. For a minute she kind of choked down. That's when we heard the music.

Around the big circle driveway came a truck — a large truck — and it was hauling a whole band. As it came on around the circle, the driver started squeezing the horn and a man was beating a drum like he was trying to kill it. Every man on that truck started blowing or beating something.

I heard a loud crashing noise down towards the stables and saw Old Fooler booger and jump right through the corral. He was plumb wild and didn't know where to go. He ran this way and that but there was always some wedding guests in his way. Finally I reckon he must've spotted me and Wrangler because he came tearing around the swimming pool scattering people everywhere. He ran right up beside us. He was shaking as bad as Myrna.

Suddenly he kind of settled down and went to gobbling some prize-winning dahlias out of the flower bed, raising his head, snorting and shaking dirt off the roots every time he got another mouthful. Then he did it. There wasn't any hope now. It was all done. I don't really think Old Fooler meant it as an insult. I just think he was plain scared into it at the sight of all this society. He lifted his tail and took a big dump right out on the patio with a pure white flower hanging out each side of his mouth.

There is not another thing to tell about old Wrangler's wedding day except this — we left.

Fifteen

Now six dollars and eighty-four cents is lots of money if you're well fed and know where you can get another meal. But it ain't much in four days without either. As soon as the word got to the Inn they kicked us right out. We moved to the edge of town, slept in our bedrolls and ate cheese and crackers every day like it was pure honey.

We went into town and started asking around for a ranch job. Seemed like everybody was well supplied.

One feller asked me why we didn't draw welfare payments. I didn't exactly understand what it was and I knew less after I talked to the Welfare people. We were offered a job in a filling station, but we didn't even have a social security card. I tried to find that vice-president to borrow one of his. He must have been out of town.

Finally we went to an employment agency. The man said, "Tomorrow's Friday. We have a client coming in who needs a couple of cowboys to break out a string of broncs. Will that be all right?"

I said, "Listen, as hungry as we are, I'll fight six wild tigers barehanded if you'll let me eat the remains."

"All right then, be here at two o'clock tomorrow afternoon and we'll see what we can do."

It was a long time till then. That night I tried to eat some of Old Fooler's oats. It wasn't that he was stingy. It was just that I couldn't get them down with him looking at me.

Wrangler said, "You've heard that song, ain't you, about the hobo who was so hungry he could eat grass. Well, I'm so empty I could eat the ground it grows in."

"This here ground's too full of rocks."

"Yeah," he said, "I done tried it."

Two o'clock finally did come. It took all the strength we had left to climb the stairs up to the second story. We went in and sat down. At two-thirty this rancher still hadn't showed. I was too weak to ask the smiling secretary if something had gone wrong. In fact, I could only smile back at her with one side of my mouth.

Right about three o'clock the man who ran the office walked in with the rancher.

That is right! It was Jim Ed Love!

Weak as he was, Wrangler jumped and ran to the window. The only thing that stopped him from jumping out was the fact he got tangled up in a bunch of those venetian blinds.

I dragged him away from the window saying, "It wouldn't do you no good to jump, Wrangler. We ain't but two stories up. All you'd do is break a bunch of bones."

He stopped kicking. We both looked at Jim Ed. He smiled and stuck his belly out over his fancy silver and turquoise belt buckle.

"You boys look like you've had a fine time. A *fine* time."

We just stood and swallered air.

"How about us going down the street here and getting a great big juicy sirloin steak with potatoes and hot gravy to boot?" Jim Ed said.

Us two ex-city slickers just followed him down the stairs rubbing our growling bellies and licking our lips.

The One-Eyed Sky

One

THE COW lifted her muzzle from the muddy water of the tank. She must go now. Her time was at hand. She could feel the pressure of the unborn between her bony hips. With the springless clicking tread of an old, old cow she moved out towards the rolling hills to find a secluded spot for the delivery.

It was late July and the sun scared in at her about an hour high. The moistureless dust turned golden under her tired hoofs as the sun poured soundless beams at each minute particle of the disturbed earth. The calf was late — very late. But this being her eighth and last she was fortunate to have conceived and give birth at all.

The past fall the cowhands had missed her hiding place in the deep brush of the mesas. If found she would have been shipped as a canner, sold at bottom prices and ground into hamburger or Vienna sausage. Not one of the men would have believed she could make the strenuous winter and still produce another good whiteface calf. She had paid the ranch well, this old cow . . . seven calves to her credit. Six of them survived to make the fall market fat and profitable. The coyotes took her first one. But she had learned from that.

She turned from the cowtrail and made her way up a little draw. Instinct guided her now as the pressure mounted in her rear body. It was a good place she found with the grass still thick in the draw and some little oak brush for shade the next sweltering day. The hills mounted gradually on three sides and she would have a down-grade walk the next morning to the water hole. She had not taken her fill of water, feeling the urgency move in her.

She found her spot and the pain came and the solid lump dropped from her. It had not taken long. She got up, licked the calf clean and its eyes came open to see the world just as the sun sank. It would be long hours now before the calf would know other than the night.

It was a fine calf, well boned and strong, good markings. In just a little while she had it on its feet. The strokes of her tongue waved the thick red hair all over. With outspread legs it wobbled a step and fell. She licked some more. Again the calf rose and this time faltered its way to the bag swelled tight with milk.

The initial crisis was over, but as the old cow nudged the calf to a soft spot to bed it down, her head came up and she scented the air. Something was there. As the calf nestled down with its head turned back against its shoulder, the old cow turned, smelling, straining her eyes

into the darkness. There was a danger there. Her calf
was not yet safe. Nature intended her to eat the after-
birth, but now there would be no chance. She stood
deeply tired, turning, watching, waiting.

Two

THE COYOTE howled and others answered in some far-distant canyon. It was a still night. The air was desert dry. It made hunting difficult. It takes moisture to carry and hold a scent. Her four pups took up the cry, hungry and anxious to prey into the night.

She, too, was old and this, her fourth litter, suffered because of it. She was not able to hunt as wide or as well as in past years. The ribs pushed through the patched hair on all the pups. They moved about, now and then catching the smell of a cold rabbit trail. Two of the pups spotted prairie mice and leaped upon them as they would a fat fowl, swallowing the rodents in one gulp. It helped, but still they all felt the leanness and the growling of their bellies.

The old coyote turned over a cow chip and let one of the pups eat the black bugs underneath. They could survive this way, but their whole bodies ached for meat.

They moved up to the water hole as all living creatures of the vast area did. The old one had circled carefully, hoping to surprise a rabbit drinking. But there was none. They had already worked the water hole many times before with some success, but now its banks were barren. They took the stale water into themselves to temporarily alter the emptiness.

The old one smelled the tracks of the cow, hesitating, sniffing again. Then she raised her head to taste the air with her nostrils. The pups all stood motionless heads up, waiting. There was a dim scent there. Not quite clear. The distance was too far, but there was a chance for meat. A small one indeed, but in these hard times the mother could not afford to pass any opportunity. With head dropping now and then to delineate the trail of the old cow, the old coyote moved swiftly, silently followed by four hungry pups copying her every move.

Three

EIGHT MILES to the north a cowboy sixty years old, maybe seventy — he had long ago forgotten — scraped the tin dishes, washed them briefly, and crawled in his bunk against the line camp wall. He was stiff and he grunted as he pulled the blanket over his thin eroded body. The night was silent and he thought.

Outside a horse stood in the corral. A saddle hung in a small shed. In the saddle scabbard was a .30-30 for killing varmints. If he had a good day and found no sign of strays in the mighty expanse of the south pasture he could ride on into headquarters the day after next to company of his own kind. It really didn't matter to him so much except the food would be better and the bed a little softer. That was about all he looked forward to now. Tomorrow he, too, would check the water hole for signs. He slept.

Four

SHE couldn't see them, but they were there. Their movement was felt and the scent was definite now. She moved about nervously, her stringy muscles taut and every fiber of her being at full strain. When they had come for her firstborn she had fought them well, killing one with a horn in its belly and crippling two more. But finally they had won. The calf — weak as all first calves are — had bled its life into the sand of the gully. She had held the pack off for hours until she knew the calf was dead and then the call from the blood of those to come had led her away to safety. It had been right. All her other calves, and the one resting beside her now, had been strong, healthy.

The scars showed still where they had tried to tear the ligaments from her hocks in that first battle long ago, she had been sore and crippled for weeks. A cowboy had lifted his gun to relieve her misery. But another had intervened. They roped her and threw her to the ground. They spread oil on her wounds and she recovered.

She whirled about, nostrils opening wide from the wind of her lungs. Her horns automatically lowered, but she could see nothing. She was very thirsty and her tongue hung from the side of her mouth. She should have taken on more water, but the enemy would have caught her during the birth and that would have been the end. She would have to be alert now, for her muscles had stiffened with age and the drive and speed she had in her first battle were almost gone. Then too, in the past, many parts of nature, of man and animal enemy had attacked her.

In her fourth summer, during a cloudburst when the rains came splashing earthward like a lake turned upside down, a sudden bolt of lightning had split the sky, ripping into a tree and bouncing into her body. She had gone down with one horn split and scorched. Three other cows fell dead near her. For days she carried her head slung to one side and forgot to eat. But she lived.

Later she had gotten pinkeye and the men had poured salt into her eye to burn out the disease.

And she had become angry once while moving with a herd in the fall roundup. She had been tired of these mounted creatures forever crowding her. She kept cutting back to the shelter of the oak brush and finally she turned back for good, raking the shoulder of the mighty horse. The mounted man cursed and grabbed his rope. She tore downhill, heading for the brush, her third calf close at her side. She heard the pounding of the hooves and the whirl of the rope. Deliberately she turned and crashed through a barbwire fence, ripping a bone-deep cut across her brisket. In that moment the man roped her calf and dismounted to tie its feet. She heard the bawling, whirled, charged at the man. She caught him with her horn just above the knee as he tried to dodge. She whirled to make another pass and drive the horns home. Then another man rode at her and the evil, inescapable snake of a rope sailed from his arm and encircled her neck. Three times he turned off, jerking her up high and then down hard into the earth, tearing her breath from her body until she stood addled and half blind. Then they stretched her out again and turned her loose. She had learned her lesson hard. During the stiff winters and wet spells she limped where the shoulder muscles had been torn apart.

But the worst winter of all was when the snow fell two feet deep and crusted over, isolating the herd miles from the ranch house. During the dry summer they had walked twice as far as usual to find the short shriveled grass. She and the others had gone into the winter weak and their bellies dragged in the drifts. When they tried to walk on top of the white desert the crust broke and they went down struggling, breathing snow and cold into their lungs, sapping their small strength. The icy crust cut their feet and they left red streaks in the whiteness. And the wind came driving through their long hair, coating their eyes and nostrils with ice. They'd wandered blindly, piling into deep drifts, perishing.

Finally the wagons — pulled by those same horses she

had hated so much — broke through the snow. They tailed her up and braced her and got some hay into her mouth. Once more she survived.

The old cow had a past and it showed in her ragged, bony, tired, bent, scarred body. And it showed in her ever-weakening neck as the head dropped a fraction lower each time she shook her defiance at the night and the unseen enemy.

The moon came now and caressed the land with pale blueness. It was like a single, headless, phosphorescent eye staring at the earth seeing all, acknowledging nothing. The moon made shadows and into these she stared and it would seem to move and then she would ready herself for the attack. But it didn't come. Why did they wait?

The night was long and the moon seemed to hang for a week, then the sun moved up to the edge of the world chasing the moon away.

Her tongue was pushed out further now and her eyes were glazed, but she stood and turned and kept her guard. She saw the old, mangy coyote directly down the draw facing her, sitting up on its haunches panting, grinning, waiting. It took her awhile to see the pups. They were spotted about the hills, surrounding her. But these did not worry her. They would not move until the old one did. Nevertheless she cast her dimming eyes at them, letting them know she knew — letting them know she was ready.

The calf stirred and raised its head and found the glorious world. First it must feed. She moved swiftly to it, watching the old coyote as she did so. The new one strug-

gled up, finding its way to the teat. The cow saw the muscles tense all over the old coyote. Its head tilted forward
as did its pointed ears. Then it moved from side to side,
inching closer at each turn. The pups got to their feet,
ready for the signal. But it didn't come. The old coyote
retreated. It was a war of nerves. And because the coyote
fights and dies in silence, when the time arrived there
would be no signal visible to the cow, only to the pups.

Now the calf wanted to explore. He wanted to know
into what it had been born. Already the color and the
form of plant and rock and sky were things of wonder.
There was so much to see and so little time for it. Again
the mother bedded down her calf — a heifer it was —
and soon the warm air and full stomach comforted it.

By midmorning the coyote had faked ten charges. And
ten times the cow had braced to take the old one first and
receive and bear the rear and flanking attacks until she
could turn and give contest. She knew from the past they
would all hit her at once, diving, feinting, tearing from
all sides. But if she could keep the calf from being mor-
tally wounded until she disposed of the old one they had
a chance. But with each rise in temperature, with each
drying, burning moment of the sun without water, her
chances lessened.

By noon the heat was almost blinding her. She felt the
trembling and faltering in her legs. All the old wounds
were making themselves known now and her tongue hung
down, parched and beginning to swell. Her breathing
came hard and heavy. The nostrils caked from the powdered dirt of her restlessness and her eyes filled around

the edges and watered incessantly. But the coyote waited. And so did the old cow. Life had always been a matter of waiting — waiting for the calf each year, waiting for the greenness of spring, waiting for the wind to die and the cold to quit and the snow to melt. But, win or lose, she would never see another spring. They would find her this fall and ship her away to the slaughterhouse. And if they didn't, the winter, the inexorable winter winds, would drive through her old bones and finish her. But now she had a chore, a life-and-death chore for sure. She would do her natural best.

In the middle of the afternoon she imagined she could smell the water, so near and yet so far away. She bawled out of her nearly closed throat and the tongue was black, and down the other side of her mouth thick cottonlike strings of saliva hung and evaporated in the interminable heat. Her legs had gradually spread apart and she wove from side to side, taking all her strength now just to stand. And right in the pathway to the water sat the laughing coyote beginning to move back and forth again, closer. Closer. As the sun moved lower and lower, so the coyote came nearer, lying down, looking straight at her.

The coyote lay very still, nothing moving but the pink tongue. Yellow eyes watching, glowing like suns. Ten minutes. Twenty minutes. The coyote came from the ground without warning, straight in and fast. The cow knew the others were coming too. She braced herself.

Five

THE MOTHER COYOTE followed the trail into scent range of the old cow. Her nostrils told her of the new one. Cautiously she moved up now, almost like a cat. The young tried mightily to do as well. It was no use. The quick, intense movement of the cow revealed her knowledge of their presence. They would have to wait. Methodically she went about spotting her young. She ringed the old cow in, giving soundless directions to her pups to stay put.

The scent of the birth, the calf, the old cow brought taste glands into action. The natural impulse was to attack as their stomachs drew narrow and craving. But the coyote could tell from the alertness of the old cow that an early assault would be sure death to some. The hours would be long but the cow would weaken. Much of the moisture had been drained from her body in the birth. The sun would be their ally. They could have the early

luxurious feast of the tender veal, and the lean meat of
the old cow would last for days — even with the vultures
and the magpies to contend with. She could fatten and
strengthen the pups and make them ready for mating as
her mother had done her. Yes, her mother had been a
good teacher and she had learned well. She had been
taught to hunt under rotten logs, cow chips and anthills
for insects in case of hard times. The field mouse had often
saved her from starvation. The lowly grasshopper had
filled her belly many times and given her strength to catch
larger, tastier game. She learned to steal into a hen yard,
make a quick dash, throttling the fowl and escaping before the rancher could get his guns. All of these things she
had taught or was teaching her own. But now must come
the ultimate lesson — how to down and kill an animal
weighing as much as fifteen of their own kind. Besides,
they were desperate in their near-starvation.

The old coyote took the main chance in locating herself
in the path of the water hole. This was the weak point
and she must handle it with care, cunning and courage.
She could not fail, for they too would weaken in the long
vigil.

She carried a .30-30 slug in her belly from the past.
She only felt it on cold or hungry nights. Her tail was
shortened and ugly at the end. Her ear was split and
torn. A scar ran across her back. One foot was minus two
toes.

The ear and tail wounds had come about at the same
time. She had learned a hard lesson from this action.
She was almost grown then and hunted with the rest of

the litter. They had stopped behind a clump of bear-grass, watching the pickup truck circle slowly. They had seen these things before, but no danger had threatened. Suddenly the thing stopped. From its back dropped six large, running hounds. Two teams.

The coyotes moved out too late. Instinct split them in three directions. But the hounds had their speed, and in less than a quarter of a mile each team had downed one of the brood. She alone escaped. On a little rise she whirled watching the hounds bear down on her brother and sister, crushing the life away with their awful fanged jaws. She sailed down from the hill and at full speed crashed into the nearest team, knocking them loose and giving her brother a chance to rise. But it didn't work. Two of the hounds flung the wounded one against the earth again. The third gave chase. She strained away in terror, knowing she could not compete with its size and strength. The hound reached for her throat but missed her and ripped the ear apart instead. They both rolled in a choking spurt of dust. As she rose, the hound clamped her tail. She broke free leaving a humiliating part of herself in his jaws. The chase was more uphill now, and she learned that hounds slowed on that sort of run and never again was she caught on the level or going downhill. She escaped. Alive. Wiser. Alone.

She learned to respect the metallic wheeled things for another reason. She had watched one from a safe distance, as far as hounds were concerned, and suddenly a black something stuck from it and then something struck her in the belly, knocking her over and down. It had been close. She bled badly inside and by the time the bleeding clotted she was very weak from hunger. All that saved her was the finding of a wounded antelope dragging itself into the tall grass of the prairie to die. But now she could smell a gun from a considerable distance. They would not hurt her again in this manner.

Her first sister had eaten poison and died before her eyes. They would not slay her in this vile way, either.

The scar on her back had come from one of those men who whirl the rope and ride horses. She was looking in a sheep pasture for a lamb to carry to her first litter of pups. She was so intent on her job she did not see the cowboy coming through the gate some half mile distant. But as he neared she felt him even before she cast her glance back over her shoulder. He came on full speed on a fast quarterhorse, whirling the rope. She did not know what it was, but she felt its danger as she did that of a gun. He was upon her and she heard the whirr of the rope mingled with the ground-jarring thump of hooves. She hit the many-wired sheep fence without slacking speed. She went through, tearing her back on the vicious barbs. Her neck was sore and twisted for many days. But she lived to hunt again.

The worst of all were the steel jaws the men put in the earth. Once, when she had been hungry, the scent of hog cracklings, and also the urine of one of her own, came to her. Bait. This gave her the confidence to inspect even though the faint scent of man was intermingled. The jaws had grabbed her as she vainly leaped away. She struck the end of the chain where it ran up out of the ground and

tightened between the trap and the heavy rock that an-
chored it. She fought wildly and in great pain for a while,
gnawing at her foot until exhaustion stilled her violent
action.

She studied the rusty, hard, impersonal steel. It had
her. But if she was to die she would do it on the mesa —
her home. Foot by painful foot, yard by wrenching yard,
she dragged the rock. The man had intended her to hang
the trap in some brush flexible enough to keep from tearing the foot loose. It hung, all right, hundreds of times,
but never for long.

It took her two days to get to the edge of the mesa. The
foot was swollen almost to the knee joint now and her yellow eyes were red from suffering. Then the stone hung
between a crack in the rocks. She fell off the other side
and rolled down the rough boulders. The trap and a part
of her foot remained in the rocks.

She lived again, less able than before.

Under the recent rising of the staring moon the coyote
studied the old cow. It was obvious she was weakening.
Soon she would lie down and then . . . but the old cow
stood and at the break of day she suckled her young, looking straight at the coyote and shaking her head in answer
to the coyote's slavering jaws. The coyote moved in now,
taunting, teasing, draining another ounce of strength
from the old cow.

The sun came soon, hot and red, striking the old cow
in the side of her head. The pups squatted and waited
with hunger pounding at their every nerve.

By midday the old coyote could feel the muscles trembling and jerking with weakness in her forelegs and the stomach walls seemed glued together, devouring themselves. She now badly needed water and food. At times the earth diffused into the molten rays of the sun and it looked as if the cow had dissolved. At other moments she bunched her muscles imagining the cow attacking. She sat with her tongue out and an eternal laughing expression in all her face except the eyes. They seared through the sun's rays, hungrily, with a quiet desperation and sureness.

The old cow's head was dropping now. She was slipping fast. But still she stood and every time the coyote moved in her snake-track advance the cow raised her head a little and tossed the pointed swords.

There was no backing out now. No changing of plans. The old mother coyote and her brood would soon be so weakened they would surely fall prey to one of their many worldly enemies. Survival now meant the death of the old cow.

The coyote drew in its dry tongue and dropped it again into the dry air and waited. The sun moved on and the old cow's legs spread a little more. The coyote could see her weaving and straining to stay upright. The tender, living veal of the calf lay folded up beside her.

Now the time was present. She sent her message of alertness to her pups. They stood ready, watching, muscles bunched, hearts pounding above the strain of hunger, thirst and heat. She moved forward and lay down to deceive the old cow. Motionless she waited and waited more. All of her being cried to lunge forward, but still she waited. She had decided on the cow's muzzle. She would dart in between the horns, locking her fangs in their breathing softness, and hang on until the aid of her pups downed the old cow. Then? It would be over shortly. A bit torn here and there and the loss of blood would finish her. Then the feast.

The burning eyes of the old coyote and the old cow were fixed on each other now. They both knew what they must do. The old coyote sent the unseen, unmoving signal to her pups and she came from the ground at the same instant, aiming straight and swift between the horns of the old cow.

Six

THE MAN arose from the bunk as stiffly as he had crawled into it. It was not quite daybreak. He clothed himself and pulled hard to get his boots on. He built a fire in the squatty iron stove and put the coffeepot on. Then he washed his face and hands in cold water. He placed a skillet on the stove by the coffeepot. Methodically he sliced thick chunks of bacon from the hog side. He took the last of the sourdough batter, tore small balls from it, placing them in a dutch oven on the stove. This done he rolled a smoke, coughing after the first puff. Soon he had a large tin cup of scalding coffee. Another cigarette, another cup. Then he ate. He wiped up the syrup on his plate with his bread. He washed the utensils and put them back on the shelf. He, or someone else, would be here another time. He went out to the corral.

If he was lucky this day and found no strays he could head for the main ranch house tomorrow morning, or if the moon was good he might ride on in tonight. He had two horses here. One ran in a small horse trap adjoining the corrals. The other he had kept up for the ride today.

He brushed his horse's back with his hand and under his belly where the cinches would fit to be sure nothing was lodged in the hair that would cut or stick. He bridled and saddled, put on his chaps and spurs and led the horse up a few steps before mounting. He rode him around the corral several times to limber him up. Then he dismounted, opened the gate, got back on, and rode south just as the sun was melting the night.

It was eight miles in a beeline to the water hole. If there was a stray in the huge pasture it would be nearby. He would probably have a twelve-mile ride, what with checking out the sign in the draw and gullies.

The sun was up now, hot for so early in the morning. It was the kind of day that made all living creatures seek shade. Well, he had always wanted a little place with lots of shade trees and water. Especially water. It wouldn't matter how big it was if there was just plenty of water. He would never forget the drought that had sent his family to the final sheriff's sale and moved them from their ranch into a tent on the edge of the little western town to take other folks' laundry, charity, handouts. His pa had already loaned him out to local ranchers. So, he just took a steady job with one of them. At first he worked only for his board and blanket. He gardened, he milked, he shoveled manure out of the barns. He patched roofs. He rebuilt corrals. He chopped a whole year's supply of firewood. He ran rabbits in holes and twisted them out with the split end of a barbwire.

And then the drought was over and the grass and cattle came back to the land. He was promoted to horse wrangler which only meant one more chore. He was up before anyone in the morning riding into the horse pasture, bringing in the day's mounts for the cowboys. But things finally got better. His boss saw him top out a waspy bronc and he was allowed to ride with the men. He got five dollars a month and felt proud. Mighty proud. He learned the ways of the range and the handling of cattle and horses. And at the age of seventeen he could draw down twenty dollars a month with room and board. By the time he had worked on ten or twelve different outfits and reached the age of twenty-five he could demand and get thirty dollars a month. Things weren't all bad.

Then a fellow cowboy with a talent for talk convinced him they were in the wrong business.

"Now look here, Snake" (that was his name at the time from being bitten by a rattlesnake), "we're makin' thirty dollars a month, right?"

"Yeah."

"Well, how much you figure a broke-out saddle horse would bring?"

"Oh, round thirty, forty dollars."

"There you are. Now, if a man could ride out say eight or ten a month?"

"I'll have to get a pencil. Besides where you goin' to get that many horses and how much you got to give for them?"

"That's just the deal. Up north in the rough country there's hundreds of wild horses. Now, I had some experience at catching them boogers when I was a kid. We're crazier than hell stayin' around here when we can get rich on our own."

So, he took all he had, two hundred and ten dollars, two head of saddle horses, one saddle, four used ropes and moved north with the talkin' cowboy. The money went fast. It was used to buy packmules and supplies.

They pitched camp and started riding the hills and canyons for sign. The horses were there, all right. But a man could ride all day and never actually see anything but tracks. They were wilder than deer by a whole lot. So the two cowboys set to work building brush corral traps in the narrow part of some canyons on the trail to the watering places. Then they built a round pole corral near camp to break the horses out. It took some wild reckless riding to pen these animals but pen some of them they did. Then they found the horses fought like bobcats and it took some doing just to get a rope on one and snub him up. It was impossible to drive them, so they tied a twisted rawhide garter on one leg. The circulation was cut off and the leg became numb and useless. It wasn't so hard to handle them then.

That was only the beginning of their troubles. When they castrated the studs, half of them died. Most of the rest lost their spirit and became dead-headed and listless.

After a good try they drifted out of the rough country ahead of the winter snow. They had two half-broken mares. But it beat walking because without them that's exactly what they would be doing. Well they went back — at thirty a month — to the cow-punching job they had left. He started saving again. Finally a rancher offered him a foreman's job at thirty-five a month and he could run as many head of his own cattle as he could acquire.

After a few months, when he had some cash to go on, he made his move. He began trading with the Mexicans. A few dollars down, a worn-out saddle, an old rifle and so on were his barter goods. In three years he had built his herd up to sixty head of cows, twelve steers and two bulls. They were a mixed lot and they were his, but the land they ranged on was not. He still couldn't figure why his boss had been so generous. Another thing he couldn't figure out was why the owner and two of his hands did so much riding without him. He didn't ask questions because it looked like a man would be a fool to tinker with good times. They were mighty scarce.

His boss sent him to a roundup over west at a neighboring ranch. His job was to check out any of their strays and deliver them back to the home range. It was a big outfit and the roundup went on for several days. The last of the work was done right at headquarters. The cowboys ate at the cookhouse. There was a pretty little brownheaded girl doing the cooking. Fine tasty chuck it was. She was the owner's daughter, Nelda.

Well, he kept eyeballing her and she kept glancing back. He was pretty good-looking at that time . . . in a rough, healed-over way. The aging and scars of the tough life hadn't taken hold yet. On the last day before he started home with his gather he asked her for a date, and he damn near fainted when she accepted.

He borrowed a buggy and picked her up late Saturday afternoon. They went to a dance at the schoolhouse. She was all decked out in a long, flimsy, turquoise dress that hugged her up close around the waist and bosom. Her hair just sparkled like her brown eyes and that was like a fall sun striking new frost on a golden aspen leaf. He was so scared and so cockeyed proud that he danced every set with her, even though he had a heck of a time fending off the other cowboys.

About four o'clock in the morning a little before day-break when the music was slow, he walked outside and leaned her up against the building. While the coyotes howled out in the prairie he pulled her up hard and said: "I . . . I love you. I sure do."

Although she didn't say anything she let him know how she felt with her arms and her eyes. Sweet.

They went steady then. His luck just kept running. He got into a poker game with a bunch of mining and timber men and won six thousand dollars. That was more money than he had seen all his life put together. He couldn't wait to get over and tell Nelda.

They rode together in the hills and he loved her and she loved him. He told her about the money and how it was not only burning a hole in his pocket but was burning right smack through his leg.

"Snake," she said, "you've got a good start on a herd and the Larking place is for sale. We wouldn't owe more than eighteen thousand."

Eighteen thousand dollars! It scared him. It was beyond him. He would never make it. He just couldn't take on a woman like her, the daughter of a big rancher, owing that kind of money.

Well, he got drunk in town and didn't show up for work. The boss fired him and told him to come and get his cows, at the same time he said there would be no hurry about it. Somehow it didn't make sense.

Snake stayed in town that fall and on into the winter trying to make up his mind what to do. In the meantime the money was going steadily out for whiskey and gambling.

The winter came and a blizzard hit. Most of his cattle walked off into deep drifts of snow and froze to death. By the time he sobered up it was spring and he was broke.

Then the law came and took him. His ex-boss was right there shaking his head and saying he couldn't believe it, after all he had done for him. They railroaded him and now he knew that he had been a blind and a cover-up for the rancher's thievery. He got a year and a day. After three dreary months inside the prison wall he planned to kill the man who sent him there, but then they put him out on the prison farm and he reasoned it wasn't worth it.

He didn't return to the home country for a long time after his release. Nelda married someone else and he kind of regretted he had been so undecided.

He tried a lot of things after that, plunging hard to come back — prospecting, timber leasing, nothing worked out. He was trying to keep from going back to punching cows. He took a job as a dude wrangler in Yellowstone Park. His natural friendliness, his knowledge of horses and everything attracted a lot of business. He had several chances to marry rich widows and cowboy-smitten girls. But he never could decide when the time came. He had heard that all was not roses and sweet violets with the rich dames. A man had to go around with his hand out all the time.

At last, though, he chose to take on this woman from St. Louis. She had come right out and told him she would buy and pay for a ranch, stock it in his name and put some money in the bank in the same manner.

Then he got drunk in Pony, Montana, on bootleg whiskey. It poisoned him and he was laid up out of his head for sixty days. The doctors almost gave up on him. By the time he came to and acquired strength enough to walk and talk, the widow had disappeared. The wrangler who had taken his job ran off to Mexico with her. If only a man could ever make up his mind at the right time he would have this world singing *his* songs he figured.

He kept trying and bumming around into one thing and another. He damned near starved. The years were beginning to show. Finally he returned to his old country and the only thing he really knew — punching cows. The wages were one hundred and twenty-five dollars a month and board. That was tops, as high as he could go in his profession. It was a job that took guts, natural skill, and understanding of the earth and its animals, both wild and domestic, though the present wages wouldn't buy as much as twenty dollars had in his youth. But there he was now riding the draws around the water hole look-ing for sign and finding none.

It was midafternoon and hot. If he turned back now he could make it in a little after dark, saddle a fresh horse and go on into headquarters. It was three days till pay-day. He could take his check, go into town, buy a new pair of jeans, a new rope, maybe a new hat. If he was careful he might have enough left over to get a little drunk and maybe even play a little poker. He really needed a pair of new boots but anything worth working in cost between forty and fifty dollars so he would just have to wait till next payday — or the next.

He decided to go on and check the water hole just in case he had missed something. It would cost him another night in the line camp but, after all, what was one more night alone to him? He saw the usual sign of wild life and was surprised to find the day-old tracks of a cow. One lonely cow. She must have strayed in here to calve, he thought. He could tell by the way her hooves splayed out and by the withered cracks around the edges that she was an old cow.

As he followed her tracks up the trail he noticed that a coyote and four pups had been ahead of him. Probably went right on, he thought, and then an uneasiness came over him. Man, it was hot. He pulled his hat back and wiped the sweat from his forehead and out of his narrow sun-washed eyes. The cow had turned off across a small ridge and he saw the tracks of the coyotes do the same. Pretty soon he felt the horse bunch under him. The head came up and the ears pitched forward. He thought he heard a sound, a cow bawling maybe, but he wasn't sure. He got down and tied the horse to a bush.

He removed the .30-30 from the scabbard and started easing forward. He was slow in his movement because of the stiffness from the long day in the saddle and many years of breaks and bruises. Then he was on his belly crawling forward feeling an excitement that he couldn't define. It was more than the hunter's blood surging now.

He raised up carefully from the side of a yucca plant. He saw the old cow first and then, slowly, one at a time, he located the coyotes. They hadn't seen or heard him yet because of the dryness and lack of wind.

He eased the rifle and sighted down it at the old mother coyote as she moved forward. Just as he started to pull the trigger she lay down right out in front of the old cow. For some reason strange to him he held his fire.

Seven

In the little hollow where the man, the coyotes, the cow and her calf lay there was concentrated the most life for miles in every direction. Five miles to the north and west in the cedar- and piñon-covered hills twenty-six buzzards circled and lighted on the remains of a doe downed two days before by a mountain lion that lay now in the coolness of the rocks with a full belly; to the east another pack of coyotes was desperately stalking a herd of swift antelope with no luck at all.

A hawk circled curiously above the draw with the man and the animals, smelling meat. The land itself was covered sparsely with buffalo and grama grass and, everywhere, the yucca plants bayoneted the sky. Now and then in meandering, meaningless lines, the land was cut by wind and water erosion forming a rolling, twisted terrain that on the face of a man would have portrayed deep torment.

The man felt the trigger of the rifle with his finger. The hammer was thumbed back. His cheek lay hot and sweating along the stock. The sights were centered on the thin rib cage of the coyote lying so very still. He could tell by the torn, powdered earth around the old cow, standing, swaying so weakly with far-drooped head, that she had held them at bay a long number of hours now.

His eyes raised again and counted the pups. One shot would do it. He must have killed two or three hundred of these animals, these varmints, these predators. He was a good shot. He would not miss. His eyes were in the second sight that comes briefly to older men. He could see almost as good as he could at twenty-one. His stomach was hollow. And he thought vaguely that it had been many hours since he had eaten or drunk. It came to him then that the creatures before him had been much longer without repast.

A sudden admiration came over him for the old, hungry, thirsty coyote and the old hungry, thirsty cow eying each other in the golden, blazing, dying sun. His duty, his real job, was to kill the old coyote and as many of her young as possible and drive the old cow to water, carrying the calf across the swells of his saddle for her. In a day or two she would have her strength back, then he could drive her on to the main herd. That was his job. But he didn't move and all of his long life came to him now as he studied what he saw before him.

The old coyote knew what she must do and she was doing it with every particle of cunning, courage and instinct in her emaciated body. Her pups must be fed and she must, too, if she was to survive and finish their training.

And the old cow had long ago reconciled herself to her fate. She would stand and fight — win or die.

The indecision was not theirs. This trait was his and had always been so.

Time became a vacuum in the floating dust. The bawling of the old cow, just a whisper now, came to him. The coyote lay like dry wood. The pups watched her, their bodies slowly evaporating in the ceaseless sun. It was everything.

His lungs ached from the shallow breathing, but still he could not move the finger that fraction of an inch that would end it. Time. Timeless time.

Then the old coyote attacked as if hurled from the earth. The pups charged down. The man fired but the bullet struck into the shoulder of one of the pups instead. The momentum carried it forward and down and over. It kicked its life away. He raised the gun and fired again. The hindquarters of another pup dropped. He levered another shell and shot it through the head.

As the old coyote came in, lips peeled back, fangs sharp and anxious, the old cow pulled a tiny ounce of strength from her heart — a little reserve she had saved for her young. She shuffled forward to meet the terrible threat.

The sound of the shot had caused the old coyote to veer just a fraction at the last thrust, and it was just enough. The lightning-splintered horn of the old cow drove between the lean ribs and she made one upward swing of her head. The horn tore into the lungs and burst the arteries of the chest apart. The coyote hung there. The cow could not raise her head again. She fell forward crushing at the earth. When she pulled her head and horns away the coyote clinked her yellow, dying eyes just once. It was over.

The other two pups ran out through the brush. They were on their own now.

The calf got to its feet and sucked a little milk from the mother's flabby bag. The man went back to his horse wondering why he had shot the pups instead of the old one. For a moment he had known. But now the knowledge was gone.

In a little while as the sun buried itself in the great ocean of space behind the earth the old cow, her calf at her side, stumbled downhill to water.

My Pardner

One

AFTER twenty-odd years, the image of Boggs is just as clear as the day he came walking towards me with his head leading his body a few inches. His skinny legs were bowed like a bronc rider's, but he wore the bib overalls of a farmer and a dirty old brown hat that flopped all over. Both boots were run over in the same direction, so he leaned a little to the left all the time. His nose was big and flat, and his mouth so wide it turned the corners of his face.

As he moved closer, I could see that there was only one crystal in his thin-rimmed glasses. A funny thing though — he had one eye gone and the crystal was on that side, leaving a single blue eye beaming from the empty gold rim.

He swung the heavy canvas bag from his back to the ground and stuck out a hand saying, "Reckon you're my pardner Dan. Well, it's shore good to meet you. I'm Boggs."

"Howdy, Boggs," I said.

"Why hell's fire, boy, you're purty near a grown man. Your pa didn't tell me that. How old are you, boy?"

"Twelve goin' on thirteen."

"Hell's fire, I was punchin' cows with the top hands when I was your age. By the time I was fifteen I was out in Arizona mining gold."

Suddenly I felt real small. Course I didn't weigh but ninety some-odd pounds. But I'd felt pretty big a while ago when Papa had handed me the map and the three dollars and said, "It's up to you, son. I'm dependin' on you and Boggs gettin' those horses to Guyman, Oklahoma, by ten o'clock July 19th." He had gone on to explain that we'd be out on the trail nearly sixty days because every other day he wanted the horses to rest and feed so's they'd get in looking good and ready for the big sale. That was the key thing to remember: balance the moving and the stopping so the horses would pick up weight.

I looked over at the corral and counted five mules and sixteen starved, ragged-looking horses of every color. Well, Papa had more confidence than I did, but I couldn't help swelling up a little when he shook hands and said, "I ain't worried a peck." But then Papa had lots of guts. Here we were on the edge of Starvation, Texas, living in a shack that was held up by hope, on land that the drought had singled out to make an example of. Half farm, half grassland, and only half enough of either one.

At heart Papa was more of a trader than a land man. He'd traded for a hotel once in Starvation, but when the drought came a few years back, everybody left Starvation except the pensioners, the postmaster, and a few others too broke to go. Then he traded the hotel for a herd of goats, and the goats for some dried-up milk cows, and the cows for a truck, and the truck for a car. Somehow or other I liked the old Ford better than the hotel. Anyway, in between he kept something to eat on the table and Ma made it taste good.

Well lately Papa had done some more figgering. The drought of the thirties had broken and people were putting a lot more virgin land into wheat and cotton. They'd need lots of horses to plow with. Most folks still hadn't gotten used to the idea it could be done cheaper and better with a tractor. The way Papa looked at it was this: by July 19th all the wheat farmers would have their wheat in and by then the grass would be made for the stock to finish fattening on. People would feel like buying horses for the next plowing. That is if it rained in early July. The spring rains had already been good. So, Papa had started trading for livestock, and finally come up with this ugly bunch. He and Uncle Jock would head up north about a week before we were due and get the sale handbills out and so on. Uncle Jock was an auctioneer, so it wouldn't take much money to pull it off. If everything worked right, we might be able to pay the mortgage, buy some seed, and put in a crop of our own the next spring.

Boggs said, "Let's git goin', boy."

My horse was already saddled and I'd thrown the rotten old pack on the gentlest of the mules. I had two blankets, a jacket, a stakerope and a sack of dried apricots tied on it. That was all. Papa had said we could find *plenty* to eat along the way. He hadn't explained exactly how.

Boggs hung his canvas bag on the pack and fished out an old bridle. Then it dawned on me he didn't have a saddle.

I said, "Ain't you got a saddle?"

He grunted, caught a bay out of the bunch, grabbed his mane and swung up bareback. We turned them out and started across the mesquite, shinnery and grass-covered pastures to Oklahoma.

Boggs rode out in front and led the string. They weren't hard to lead, because they were in such poor shape, but riding the drag was something else. They just wanted to stop and eat all the time. I was riding back and forth every minute yelling them on. All the same I felt great again — sorta like a man must feel on his first ocean voyage.

Along about noon I could feel my belly complaining. We rode up to a windmill and watered the horses. After my horse had finished I got down and took a drink. Then I reached in the pack and got a double handful of apricots, and handed some to Boggs. He spit out his chew of tobacco, wiped his mouth, and threw in the whole batch and went to chewing.

When he finished, he said, "Boy, get up on that horse. I want to show you something." It took me kind of by surprise but I crawled up. "Now look here," he said. "Look at your knees. See how they kind of bend when you put 'em in the stirrups. Now look here," he said, walking off. "See them pore old bowed legs of mine? Why you could run a grizzly bear through there without him even knowin' it. Now ain't that a disgrace?" he said.

"I don't see as it is," I said, having always felt bowed legs to be some sort of badge of honor.

"Well, by jingos!" he said. "You don't see, boy? You don't see? Do you realize that I'm a highly educated man —havin' traveled far and wide and knowin' all about the isns and ain'ts of the world? Young feller, I'll have you know that at one time I was made a bonafide preacher. Yessir, a man of the Lord dwellin' in his own house, spreadin' the true and shinin' light. But what happened?" and he jumped around on his runover boots waving his long arms in the air. "What happened?" he shouted, putting that sky-blue eye on me. "Here's what happened," he said as he squatted down and pulled off his boots and overalls and waded out into the dirt tank. "Look," he said, "look at them legs. By jingos and hell's fire, boy, how would you like to be baptized by a preacher with a pair of legs like that?"

I burst out laughing, even though I was half scared I'd made him mad.

"There you are," he shouted, running out of the water. "That's another thing that happened . . . peals, barrels, tubsfull of laughter burstin' across the land. You see, Dan," he suddenly lowered his voice and it was like dragging satin over satin, "a young boy like you with his bones still growin' and shapin' should never ride a saddle. Otherwise your legs will get bent like mine. A long trip like this will doom the young sapling. Let me have that saddle, son, and save you this terrible disgrace. Grow up straight and tall like Abe Lincoln. And besides," he leaned at me with his hand in the air signaling for silence, "besides, when our duty is done I'll buy you the fanciest present this side of the pearly gate."

Well that was fancy enough for me. I just crawled down, unfastened the cinches and handed him my saddle. He threw it on his bay horse, then went over to the pack and took out a half-gallon crock jug.

"Cider" he said, tossing it over his arm and taking a long pull. "Ain't good for younguns," he said, corking the jug. "Cures the earache. Always got an earache." He rubbed one ear and put the jug back inside the bag. Then he took out a long plug of tobacco and really bit him off a chew. "Let's git goin'," he said, and we struck out.

About five hours later the horses quit. There wasn't any way to keep them all moving at once. Well, I had an inkling why. My belly was just plain gone. It had lost confidence in ever being fed again and had just shriveled up to nothing.

Boggs rode back and said, "We'll pitch camp right over there." He pointed to a dry lake bed with a heavy growth of mesquite most of the way around its edges. Off to the northeast I could see a clump of trees sitting like a motionless prairie ship in a green grass sea. I knew there was a ranch house there with beans and bacon and good black coffee, but it would be late the next day before we'd make it. Tonight we'd dine on apricots. Dried.

We unsaddled the horses. I took my rope and staked out one for a night horse. I wasn't worried about the others running off. They were too hungry. Besides, they would be easy to hem up in a fence corner about a quarter of a mile off.

I spread my blanket out and Boggs reached in his canvas bag. He had another pull of ear medicine. He fished around in the bag and came up with a coffeepot and a little dutch oven. Then he said, "Gather some wood, boy. I'll be back in a minute." He struck out in that rocking-chair walk of his, leaning to the west.

I started picking up dead mesquite limbs, watching every now and then to see what Boggs was doing. I could see him twisiting some loose wire on the corner post. I didn't know what he was up to, but if a rancher caught him we'd sure be in trouble.

He came back carrying a six-foot strand of barbwire and said, "Come on, let's git goin'."

I followed. We walked out through the mesquite. All of a sudden he yelled, "After him! After him!"

I saw a cottontail rabbit shoot out between us. I took after him feeling like a damn fool. The fastest man on earth can't catch a rabbit. Well, that cottontail wasn't taking any chances on it. He ran and jumped in a hole. I stopped, breathing hard, but Boggs just ran on past me, right to the rabbit hole. He squatted down, took one end of the wire and spread the strands about two thirds of an inch apart. Then he bent about ten inches of the other end out at forty-five degrees. He put the forked end into the hole and started twisting the wire. To my surprise the wire went right on down, and even passed the spot where the hole turned back. Then I could see him feeling his way. His eye was bugged out in concentration. His face was red and sweating. Then he gave another couple of twists and said, "Got 'em, boy. Now the secret is, *not* to bring 'em up too fast or you'll pull the hide out and they're gone. If you bring 'em up too slow then they'll get a toehold and the same thing will happen."

He backed up now and I could see the rabbit.

"Grab 'im!"

I did.

"By jingos, he's a fat one. A regular feast," he said, and he wasn't joking.

We built a nice fire and Boggs scraped the fat off the rabbit hide, then we cooked him in his own juice. I'm telling you that rabbit woke my stomach up and really put it back to work. We finished it off with a cup or two of black coffee and half a dozen apricots. The world was all of a sudden a mighty fine place.

I leaned back on my elbow and watched the flat rim of the prairie turn to bright orange. High above, some lace clouds got so red for a minute I thought they would just drop down and burn a man up. Then the cool violets and purples moved in and took over. Bullbats came and dived in the sky in great swift arcs, scooping the flying insects into their throats. The crickets hummed like a Fordson tractor, and away off the coyotes started their singing and talking howl.

Then Boggs said, "Boy, you ever been to Arizona?"

"No."

"Course you ain't. But you will. That's a great country, boy. That desert and all that gold just waitin' to be dug."

He went on a little while and I looked at the sky full of stars and my eyes got heavy just trying to see past the first bunch. Then his voice came again, "I'll tell you all about Arizona one of these nights, boy, but right now my ass is too tired."

I could hear the horses grazing nearby, snorting now and then, slowly in contentment. The fire was a small red glow teasing the night goodbye. I slept.

Two

"Let's git goin', boy."

I sat up in my blankets.

"Here." He handed me a cup of hot coffee, and kicked dirt over the fire.

It was just breaking day. I swallered the scalding stuff and tried to stand up. This took some doing. I was sore and stiff in every joint, but that wasn't what bothered the most; it was my hind end. The rawboned back of the saddle horse had rubbed my rump like grating cheese. I had to walk with my legs spread apart. It was not a good condition for horseback riding.

The sun got hotter. My setter got rawer. Every little bit I'd slide off and walk, but the insides of my legs were galled so bad I couldn't keep up with the slowest of our horse herd. There was nothing to do but get on and go.

By eleven o'clock I was hurting so bad, and the sun was so hot, I got somewhat ill-tempered. I was cussing Boggs,

not altogether under my breath. "You old liar and con-
niver. You old nut-wut. You old . . ." It eased my pain.

By two that afternoon we pulled up to the trees. There
was a water tank about fifty yards long and a windmill
pumping at each end. But the ranch house had long been
unoccupied. It looked like now it was occasionally used
as a temporary camp for cowboys. It was a disappoint-
ment. While not thinking about my sore bottom, and
when not cussing Boggs, I thought about the beans and
bacon, hot gravy and biscuits we'd have had at the
rancher's table. I just got down and lay in the shade and
listened to my belly growl.

After the horses watered we turned them all loose in a
little horse trap where the grass was coming good.

"Reckon there's any rabbits around here?" I asked
Boggs, chewing on an apricot.

"Might be," he said, looking in the tank.

"There ain't no rabbits taking a swim in that tank," I
said.

"You're right, boy, but I'm tellin' you there's some catfish in there."

"Catfish?" I said, bolting up out of the shade.

"Yessirree Bob."

Then I settled back down. "Well, we ain't got no way
to catch 'em. Guess we better get to lookin' for a rabbit."

"Now look here, boy, you're givin' in too easy. We're
goin' to have an ample amount of rabbit before this trip
is over anyway, so let's try doing a little thinkin'. It's all
right to go through life just plain feelin', that's fine, but

when your old gut is cryin' 'hungry' to your soul, it's time to think. You hear? Think!"

Well, we walked around the yard. If you could call his bowlegged and my wide-spraddled motions walking. We went into the ranch house; nothing but an empty table, cupboard and four chairs. Out in a shed, we found some tools, old and rusty, a can of axle grease, and a stack of empty feed sacks tied in a bundle.

Boggs said, "Look here, the great gods above done smiled down on us poor sinners. By jingos, boy, we're in for a treat." He gathered up the sacks and out we went.

After untying and splitting the sacks, he spread them out on the ground and began sewing them together in one big sheet. Then he tied some rocks along the bottom, put sticks on each end for handles and we had us a dandy good seine.

Boggs went back in the shed for a minute. "Here, boy," he said, handing me a can of axle grease.

"What's that for?"

"Rub it on your hind end."

I just stood there holding it in my hand.

"Well, go on," he said, "we ain't got much time."

I rubbed it on. It was sticky and left me a little embarrassed when I walked, but it did ease the pain.

"Pick you out a couple of them sacks to ride on tomorrow."

I did.

"Now, come on, boy. We're wastin' time."

Boggs told me to go to the deep end and start throwing rocks into the tank and yelling. He said this would booger

the fish into the shallow water so we'd have a chance at
them.

About middle ways down, we shucked our clothes and
waded in. I sure was glad I had applied the axle grease in
the right place. That water would have really finished
chapping me. I pretty nearly choked to keep from laughing at Boggs' bowlegs until he got them under water. The
seine was spread and he told me to keep the bottom just a
little ahead of the top so the fish couldn't get underneath.

"Now, boy, move in steady to the corner and when I
yell, come out with the bottom first and hold tight. Then
give a big heave out on the bank."

We moved along.

"Haawwww!"

Up we heaved. Sure enough there were seven or eight
nice cats, three perch and a goldfish. I didn't heave quite
enough and two of mine fell back, but the next trip
through we got another good catch and Boggs said, "Hell,
that's all we can eat, so let's go swimming." He put the
fish in a wet gunnysack and we took a fine cooling swim.

When we crawled out the sun felt good for a change.
Just when I thought I was going to faint from hunger and
the extra exercise, Boggs said, "Boy, get out there and get
a bunch of wood."

I went after it. When I got back with the first load he
had dug a hole about a foot deep and a yard long. He
built a fire in this hole and I kept packing wood for it.
After the fish were cleaned and wrapped in some pieces of
brown paper sacks we'd found in the shed, he mixed up a
batch of mud and rolled them in it. When all the wood

had burned down to glowing coals, he buried the fish in them.

We waited and we waited.

"Don't you think they're done, Boggs?" I asked feeling the saliva run into my mouth.

"Not yet."

"Lord, I'm starving. Looks like to me those coals have done gone out."

"Not yet."

Finally, he took one out and broke it over a rock. The baked mud fell away and there it was, the juicy white meat of the catfish. Everything was soon gone but a pile of bones cleaned as slick as crochet needles.

All the next day we let the horses rest, water and eat. We did the same. Then on the move again. The wide green tablecloth of a prairie soon turned to shinnery bushes and sand where the sun was meaner and the earth drier. We ate rabbits and apricots until the apricots were gone, and that left *just* rabbit.

Then we could see the little clumps of trees increasing in the distance, and we knew we were finally on the edge of the farm country.

We checked our map. If we were lucky, we could make it to a Mr. Street's farm before night. He was supposed to be a friend of Papa's. Papa said Mr. Street was a pure farmer and wouldn't have any pasture grass for our horses, but he would have plenty of cane bundles to give us. It was here I was to buy two hundred pounds of oats out of the three dollars and start graining our herd.

As I followed the old white horse into Mr. Street's road I finally figured out why he was behind the others all the time — one ankle was twisted just enough to make him slower. He was a stayer though. I was getting to feel friendly toward him and wouldn't have liked any of the other horses back with me.

I went up to the front of Street's house, leaving Boggs out in the road with the horses where they grazed along the bar ditch. It was a neat, white house with a paling fence around it, and a few elm trees scattered about the place. I could see a big barn, several corrals and feed stacks. Down below the house was a shack for the colored hired hands. Mr. Street was rich. I could sure tell that.

I tied my horse at the yard gate, went up to the door and knocked. It didn't feel as if anyone was home. I couldn't hear a sound. Then I knocked again and waited. Just as I raised my hand, the door opened.

"What'd you want?"

I looked up and up and sideways and all around. That door was full of woman. I felt like I was standing at the bottom of a mountain.

"Well, what'd you want?"

"Is Mr. Street in?"

"What'd you want?"

"My papa . . ."

"Your papa? What about your papa. Come on, boy, speak your piece."

"Well, uh, my papa is a friend of Mr. Street's."

"Who *is* your papa?"

"Ellis Thorpe."

"You know any Ellis Thorpe, Nate?" she said back over her shoulder.

"Yeah, used to," he said. "Ain't seen him in years."

I never saw such a woman — little bitty ankles with massive muscular legs above to hold up the rolls and rolls of blubber that ran right up under her ears and spread over her cheekbones so it made her eyes look little and mean. Sure enough they were.

"Well, what *do* you want?" she asked again.

"Papa said you might put us up and feed our horses for a day."

She went in and talked to Nate in low tones. Then she filled the door again.

"Nate says times have been hard what with overcoming the drouth and all, but he says you can bunk down at the shack with the help and you can have all the bundles you want at a nickel apiece."

"I, uh . . ."

She started to shut the door.

"Just a minute," I said and pulled out the three dollars. "I guess we'll take two bundles apiece for the horses. How much'll that be?"

"How many head you got?"

"Sixteen horses and five mules."

"Forty-two bundles at five cents." She counted on her little short fingers . . . "Two dollars and ten . . . er . . . twenty cents."

I handed her the three and she brought me eighty cents change. She slammed the door.

I felt sick. There went the grain money. I'd already started letting Papa down.

We took the horses to the corrals and started pitching them the bundles. Then Nate came out and counted them. He was a little man with a quick, jerking motion to everything he did. When he was satisfied we hadn't cheated him he said, "Tell your pa hello for me," and walked off.

Over on the other side of the corral stood four big, fat Percheron work horses. They made ours look like runts, and I began to wonder if Papa had a good idea or not.

It was almost night when we walked down to the workers' shack. Three little colored kids grinned at us from the steps. Boggs spoke to them and a man came to the open door.

"Howdy. What can I do for ya?" he asked.

"Well, Mr. Street said we could bunk with you to-night."

"Sho, sho, come in," he said. "I'm Jake."

He introduced us to his wife, Telly. She was almost as big as Mrs. Street, but somehow in a different way. There was something warm about the place.

Boggs sent me to get our blankets and his cider jug off the pack saddle. Telly sat out three cups and they all had a drink.

"Sho fine," said Jake.

"Better'n fine," Telly said.

"Best cider in Texas," said Boggs winking at them and they all busted out laughing.

Then Telly fixed us a big stack of hot cakes, and set a pitcher of black, homemade molasses on the table. I smeared a big dip of churn butter between about six of them and let the molasses melt all over. I forked three strips of sowbelly onto my plate and really took me on a bait of home cooking. Then two tin cups of steaming coffee finished it off.

A while after the eating was over the three grownups went back to that cider jug.

Every little bit Boggs would say to Jake, "Ain't you got a bad earache, Jake?"

"Sho nuff, Mr. Boggs, I do. I ain't never knowed a ear to hurt like this'n."

Telly said, "Well, you ain't sufferin' atall. Both my ears done about to fall off."

The only earache I'd ever had hurt like seventy-five. I never could figger out how these people were getting such a kick out of pain. I spread my blankets on the floor and lay down to get away from all this grown-up foolishness.

It was soon dawn again, and it was Boggs again.

"Let's git goin', boy. Leave the eighty cents on the table for Jake."

I was too sleepy to argue.

We moved the horses out fast. Then I said, "Boggs, where's the pack mule? We forgot the pack mule."

"Shhhh," he said. "Shut up and come on."

In a little while, maybe three quarters of a mile from Street's, I saw the pack mule tied to a fence. On each side of the pack saddle hung a hundred-pound sack of oats.

"Where'd you get 'em?" I asked bristling up.

"From Street."

"That's stealin!"

"No, it ain't, son. I've done him a real favor."

"How's that?" I said smartly.

"Why, boy, you ain't thinkin' again. This way him and your pa will remain friends."

I studied on it all day, but I was a full-grown man before I figured it out.

"Well, anyway that's too much for that mule to carry," I said.

"That shows how little you've been around the world, boy. That mule is plumb *underloaded*. When I was mining out in Arizona we packed four hundred pounds of ore out of the mountains. *Mountains*, you hear. This mule is at least a hundred pounds underloaded."

"Oh," I said, and we moved out with me staring that old white horse square in the rump.

Three

After a while we stopped at a little grassy spot along the road and poured out some oats. Those old horses were really surprised.

"You know something, boy?" Boggs said, filtering a handful of dirt. "This here's sand land. Watermelon land. They come on early in this soil. Fact, just about this time of June."

He raised his head kind of sniffing the air as if he could smell them. Then he got up and ambled off through a corn patch that was up just past knee-high. I sat and watched the horses eat the oats thinking what a damn fool Boggs was for figuring he could just walk off across a strange country and come up with a watermelon. I'd stolen watermelons myself, and I knew better than that.

The ponies finished their oats and started picking around at the grass and weeds in the lane. I began to get uneasy. Maybe somebody had picked Boggs up for trespassing. Then I heard singing. I listened hard. It was coming through the corn. I heard loud and clear, "When the saints . . . Oh, when the saints go marching off. Oh, when the saints . . ." closer and closer till I could see the long stringy figure of Boggs, and the watermelon he had under each arm.

"Had a little trouble finding two ripe ones. Most of 'em's still green."

I didn't say a word.

He took out his long-bladed barlow and stuck her in a melon. It went riiiiiip as it split wide apart like a morning rose opening up. I knew it was a ripe one. He cut the heart out with his knife and handed it to me. I took it in both hands and buried my head plumb to my nose in it. Good. Wet. Sweet. Whooooee.

I ate every bit of that watermelon except the seeds and rind and my belly stuck out like I'd swallered a football. Boggs didn't waste much of his either. It was a mighty fine lunch.

When we stood up to mount our horses, I said, "Boggs, sure enough how'd you know them watermelons was over there?"

"Look right there in them weeds under the fence."

All I could see was a bunch of flies buzzing around. I walked over. Sure enough there was a half-ripe watermelon that somebody had busted open the day before.

"I just figgered nobody would carry one any further than that without seein' if it was ripe. Knew they had to be close by."

"Oh."

We got our horses and rode. We soon came to the main highway to Brownfield, Texas. According to Papa's map we'd be riding along this bar ditch for a long spell now. It was late afternoon and that watermelon belly had disappeared and the usual holler place was making itself known.

We looked around and finally found an old fallen down homestead out in a cotton patch. It was vacant, and there was a lot of weeds and stuff growing around the barns and old corrals for the horses to feed on. But we still had to water them. The windmill was cut off and if we turned it on in the daylight somebody might see it and maybe have us arrested for trespassing. We had to wait for dark.

Boggs said, "Let's see if we can find a rabbit."

We'd already lowered the rabbit population of West Texas a whole lot but I was willing to thin it some more. We rode along the fencerows, all around the old place, but there wasn't a cockeyed rabbit to be found. About half a mile from the homestead we looked out over a weed-covered fence. There was a farmhouse with chickens, milk cows, chickens, some white ducks in a little pond, chickens and dogs.

"By jingos, boy, how'd you like to have some roasted chicken tonight?"

"Sure would, Boggs, but we ain't got any money."

"Money? Why only a sinner against mankind would pay money for a chicken."

"What do you mean?" I asked, feeling fingers made out of icicles grabbing my little skinny heart.

"I mean we'll procure them chickens. Now you know

the lady of that house is overworked. She's probably got six kids to look after besides her old man. All them ducks to feed, and the churnin' to do after milkin' those cows. Now it's just too much to ask of her to take care of *that* many chickens and gather *that* many eggs, ain't it?"

I started to say it was stealing, but my belly set up those growling noises again and I felt my legs trembling from hunger weakness.

"What about the dogs?" I asked.

"No bother atall. I'll take care of the dogs while you steal the chickens."

"Me?"

"You."

"Now listen . . ."

"Now you listen close and I'm goin' to tell you how to get the job done. Why hell's fire, boy, you're just the right size for such an operation."

I wondered how in the world it could make any difference to a chicken whether I weighed ninety pounds or two hundred.

"Now about them dogs. I'm goin' to go off to the right of the house and howl likc a coyote. The dogs will come out barkin' and raisin' cain at me. It'll throw everybody's attention in my direction. Get it?"

I swallered.

"Now the minute you hear me holler and the dogs start barkin' get to that henhouse. Here's the secret of chicken stealin': first, a chicken sleeps pretty sound. About the only thing that will wake 'em is one of their own takin' on. *That* you have to avoid. Be as quiet as you can gettin' into the henhouse. When you're used to the dark so you can see a chicken, grab her right by the throat and clamp down hard so's she can't make any noise. Then just stick her head under her wing. A chicken's so dumb it won't make a sound. Now as soon as this is done carry her outside and do 'er round and around in the air," he said and made a circular motion with his arms held out, "like this. She'll be so dizzy, it'll take 'er ten minutes to stand up again and that much longer to get her head out from under her wing. You can steal a whole henhouseful in twenty minutes."

"Do we want 'em all?"

"Hell's fire no, boy. Just one apiece."

Darkness came and the lights went on in the farmhouse. Every once in a while the dogs would bark. I think they heard us.

Boggs said, "Let's git goin'."

He circled off to the right of the house and I eased along to the left behind the henhouse. When the dogs started barking, I stopped. They quit for a minute and I heard that coyote Boggs hollering his head off. I dashed up to the henhouse with my breath coming in quick gasps and cold prickles just breaking out all over. I was scared but at the same time thrilled. I slipped around to the door and fumbled for the latch. The noise pierced the night like a runaway wagon. It was too late to back out now. Besides, I was too durned hungry.

I heard the chickens stir and talk a little as I went in. I stood still just a minute. My heart thumped louder than the chickens. I could make out a dark mass over on the roost. I moved as quietly as I could with my hands out-stretched. The dogs were really raising the dickens over on the other side of the house. I wondered if maybe they had Boggs down chewing on him.

Then my hand touched a chicken neck. I squeezed tight and holding her with one hand I stuck her head under her wing with the other. Outside I went. Whirl that chicken I did. I plunked her down and she just sat there like Boggs had said. This gave me confidence. In a half a minute I had another one outside on the ground all dizzy and still. Then I relatched the door. That Boggs had started me thinking tonight. I grabbed up a chicken under each arm, and sailed out of there.

Boggs got back about twenty minutes after I did.

"What took you so long?" I asked, feeling kind of important.

This seemed to rock him back for a minute, then he said, "A funny thing, boy. Just as I raised my head to let out that coyote yell, a sure-enough live one beat me to it. I just hung around a few extra minutes to see what'd happen."

The cooking took place.

The eating took place.

The sleeping with a full belly took place.

And I dreamed.

Four

WE WENT through Brownfield before sunup, right into the heart of cotton country. It stood up straight and green everywhere. In a few more weeks the hard, round boles would form. Then in the fall when they burst open into the white white of ripe cotton the fields would fill with bent-over pickers dragging long canvas bags behind them and their hands snaking cotton from the vine to the sack. Wagons by the hundreds would pull it to the gins, and the gins would hum day and night for a brief spell, cleaning and baling the cotton for shipping and sale all over the world. Now, it was still, and hot, and green.

The people in the autos traveling parallel to us all waved. I guessed it had been a long time since they had seen a remuda of horses on the move. All the horses, except the old gray, were beginning to pick up flesh. Just the same I couldn't help worrying some. In the first place, if that thieving Boggs got us in jail, our time schedule

would be thrown off, and one half day late would be just
the same as a month. I couldn't figger Boggs out. One
minute he'd be preaching and the next he was stealing.
Sometimes his speech was like a school professor's, and
then like an uneducated dunce. On the other hand, I
would have starved nearly to death without his help. We
were hungry most of the time anyway. Besides worrying
about letting Papa down, all I could think about was getting enough in my belly to last a whole day.

We moved on through Meadow, Texas, and then out to
the edge of Ropesville. We had a two-day hold up here if
we wanted it. There was a patch of heavy grass by the
road where a sink hole had held back some extra moisture
from the spring rains. We decided to take a chance on
the horses grazing alone on the road while we did a little
exploring. This was risky because if someone took a notion to impound our horses, we were done. It'd cost five
dollars a head to get them out. That would be impossible
to raise in time to make the sale, but Boggs had said,
"Our luck's holdin', son. You can't beat luck — even with
thinkin'. The odds are that no one'll think but what the
owner is keepin' his eye right on 'em. You got to be
willin' to take chances. The way to survive this world is
knowin' when to duck. That time generally comes when
a man has made a mistake while takin' a chance. Now
you take my whole durn family. Ma for instance. She
died having me cause she didn't reckon she needed a doctor. Now my brother got killed robbin' a bank. He
walked in when two plainclothesmen were making a de-
posit. He should have watched *everybody* instead of just

the guard. That sister of mine jumped in the Arkansas River to save a drowning boy. The boy caught hold of a limb and swam out — she sank. Pa didn't do so bad. I don't reckon you can hold it against a man for gettin' choked on a piece of bear meat. By jingos, boy, you can't hold that against a man, especially since he killed that bear with his own hands wingin' a choppin' axe."

"No," I said, "you cain't."

"You're right, boy."

We cut across a pasture looking for a place to hide the horses for a couple of days. The nearest house was about a half mile away, and we had to get out of its sight.

"Looky there!"

"What?" I said.

"A rat's den!"

It was a whopper — three feet high and six or eight feet in width and length — made up of broken mesquite limbs, thorns, bear-grass leaves and cowchips, with numerous holes woven in and out.

"Rats!" he screamed into the air, throwing his long arms up as if seeking the help of the Almighty. "Rats! Rats! Rats! Oh gracious and powerful Lord give me the strength to wage battle against these vilest of creatures. Pass on to me a small portion of your power so that I may stand strong and brave through the conflict about to come upon us. Lend me some of your skill and eternal magic while I slay the carnal beasts. Guide and protect this innocent young man as he follows forth to the bugle's glorious call."

I was getting boogered and looked all around to see

what might be fixing to tear us in pieces when he jumped from his horse and handed me the reins.

"Here, boy, this is your duty. Hold the mounts that we may yet escape to wage war another day."

He raced to the large pile of trash and put a match to it. A lazy rope of smoke rose, then burst into flames. Boggs had secured a long, heavy mesquite limb and he had it drawn back in a violent gesture.

"Ah, you four-legged offspring of the devil, I have turned your own fire and brimstone against you. Seek ye now the world of the righteous."

Well, they started seeking it. Rats were fleeing the burning nest in every direction. Boggs was screaming and striking with fury. Dead rats soon covered the ground.

"There, pestilence!" he shouted as he bashed one to a pulp. "Die, evil creature of the deep. Return to your ancestor's wicked bones. Bring the black death into the world will you? Destroyer of man, of his food, of his life. Die, rats, die!"

When he could find nothing else to strike at he turned to me breathing heavily, still waving the stick.

"Rats have killed more people than all the wars combined. Did you know that, boy?"

I shook my head "no," trying to quiet the nervous horses.

"Well, they have. They are man's one mortal enemy. They live off man's labor, off his love for other things. They can't survive without man. It's a battle to the great and final death. People shouldn't fight people, they should fight rats. Here, give me my horse."

He dropped his stick on the dying fire and mounted.

"We better get out of here," I said. "That smoke will draw some attention."

"Just the opposite, if it's gone unnoticed till now we'll be safe in pasturing our horses here. Let's git goin'."

I was in such shape after the last few minutes of action that I just rode obediently along and helped gather our horses. It was almost night and that same old weakness of all day without food was upon me. It never seemed to bother Boggs, or at least it didn't show. He rammed a plug of tobacco in his mouth and chewed on it awhile. He seemed to be studying hard.

Turning to me all of a sudden, he spoke. "Boy, I'm takin' you out for a steak dinner."

"We ain't got any money."

"That's right, boy."

"Well?"

"Don't ask so many questions. Would you like a steak dinner or not? It's too late to catch a rabbit."

"Yeees," I said meekly.

Ropesville, Texas, had two tin cotton gins standing huge and sightless like blind elephants. The cotton lint from the ginning last fall still hung in dirty brown wads from the phone and light wires and in the weeds and grass around the town. It was a small place, maybe a thousand or twelve hundred people in and around the town. But it was a big town to me this night.

We tied our horses in a vacant lot off the main street. I was scared plumb silly. I had no idea how Boggs was going to get us a steak dinner without stealing it. And I just couldn't figger any way to steal it without a gun.

We marched right around to the first restaurant we came to, stepped in and got us a table.

A woman came over smiling like she meant it and said, "Good evening."

"Evenin', ma'am," said Boggs, standing and bowing. "A menu?"

"It's not necessary. My pardner and I desire one of your finest chicken-fried steaks."

There wasn't any use ordering any other kind of steak in the backwoods of West Texas in those days. They all served the one kind.

"Would you kindly put a little dab of mayonnaise on our salad? And pie? What kind of pie you want, boy?"

"Apple?"

"Apple for me, too, ma'am."

"Coffee?"

"Coffee for me and orange soda pop for the youngun."

"All right." And she went away writing.

In a little bit there was a whole table load of stuff. I stuck my fork in the steak and sawed my knife back and forth. I put a great big bite into my mouth. Whoooeee! Was it ever good. Before I hardly got it swallowed I took a big bite of the mashed potatoes on the plate and another of salad. Then when I got my mouth so full I could hardly chew I'd wash it down with a big pull of orange pop. Great goin'! For a minute I'd quit worrying about how we'd pay for it.

The time came to face up to it. Boggs was finished and so was I. The lady came over and asked if there'd be anything else.

Boggs said, "Another soda pop, coffee and the ticket, please."

Well, I drank on that soda and watched Boggs. I'd been scared plenty on this trip already, but he was really headed for the deep end now. Every once in a while he'd grab out in the air like he was crazy. Then I saw him put his hand over his coffee cup like he was dropping sugar in it. But the sugar was in a bowl.

All of a sudden he straightened up and said seriously, "Lady. Lady, come here."

The lady walked over smiling. Boggs pointed silently into his coffee cup. She looked. The smile crept off her face.

"I . . . I . . . I'll get you another cup."

"Lady," Boggs said under his breath, "I don't want any more coffee — that ecstasy has been denied me now and probably forever. One of the true pleasures of life will now raise only a ghastly memory to my mind at every thought. I feel I should bring suit against this café." Boggs rose now and so did his voice.

The other customers had stopped eating and the woman ran to a man behind the counter. He looked up, listened, and walked over to our table.

"Please, please," he said. "Just quiet down and leave. I'll take care of the check."

Boggs stood a minute with his gleaming blue eye on the man. "Very well," he said standing there with his head thrown back, "but you haven't heard the last of this yet. Boy, let's git goin'."

As I walked around the table I leaned over just a minute and looked in the coffee cup. There were two big, fat flies in there and only one had drowned.

Five

BOGGS woke me up praying. I'd slept late for once; it was nearly noon. All we had to do this day was feed and water ourselves. It didn't sound like much but it could turn into quite a chore. Anyway I heard this voice taking on. I raised up in the blankets and tried to rub my eyes open.

"Lord, now listen to me close. We're goin' to be in the land of plows and man-planted things for over eighty miles now. It's goin' to get harder and harder to live off the land. We made a promise, me and Dan, to deliver these fine horses on time and in good shape. We got to keep that promise one way or the other, Lord. All I ask of you is to help me think. And listen, Lord, if I mess up, which being one of those so-called human bein's I'm liable to do, I want you to know I ain't blamin' it on you. Amen, Lord." Then looking over his shoulder at me he said, "Mornin', boy. It's a great day. Care for a cup of coffee?"

"Uh-huh." I looked at it to see if there were any flies in it.

Then he said, "When you finish, let's go to town."

I swallered. We went.

We were riding along the highway when he spotted a big piece of cardboard leaning against the fence. He got down and cut out a couple of eight-inch squares. Then with a stubby pencil he wrote on one: I'M DEAF AND DUMB. This one he hung around my neck. On the other he wrote: I'M BLIND. This one was his. I didn't need any explanations this time to figure out what *we* were fixing to pull.

He took off his glasses and put on a pair of dark ones he had in his canvas bag. He put his floppy old hat in the bib of his overalls, pulled his yellow hair down over his forehead, and rubbed some dust on his right eyelid. When he closed it, it looked sunken like his blind one.

We tied our horses in the same alley, and started down the street carrying a large tomato can he got from the bar ditch.

"Now, boy, if anybody tries to talk to you just shake your head and make Indian sign language."

"I don't know any Indian sign language."

"They ain't nobody goin' to know the difference. Here, boy, hold my hand. Cain't you see I'm blind?"

I took his hand and walked into the lobby of the town's only hotel. I held the tomato can out in front. An old lady put down the newspaper she was reading, reached in her purse and dropped fifteen cents in the can. She rubbed me on the head saying, "What a pity."

I blinked my eyes real hard for her.

The man at the desk gave me a dime and on our way out a man and his wife stopped and watched us. The man fetched a nickel out of his pocket but his wife glared and gouged him in the ribs with her elbow. He came up with fifty cents this time.

The drugstore was next. We left there with nearly two dollars. Boggs dragged his feet along, not only looking blind, but acting like it. The grocery store was good for eighty-five cents. Then a garage for forty. A little girl with a nickel in her hand kept following us around from place to place, running out in front once in a while to stare at us. All of a sudden she ran up and dropped the nickel in the can and gave me a kiss. If my knees had been trembling before they were going in circles now. Boy, I sure wished I had time to get to know a girl who would give up a bar of candy and a kiss for a dumb boy — and a stranger at that.

We made it on down to a red brick building at the end of the street. There was a bank and a drygoods store. The bank was closed but the drygoods was worth ninety-five cents. By the time we'd covered the entire north side of the street we had fourteen dollars and sixty-three cents. We went into the alley to count it.

"By jingos, we're rich," I said. "I ain't *never* seen so much money."

Boggs smiled clean around his face. "I used to make this much in a day when I was panning gold in Arizona."

"How come you left?"

"The gold was gone."

"*All* gone?"

"Hell's fire, no, boy, not all of it, just all of it in this one spot. I'm goin' back some day. Besides, I decided to try to find my gold already coined in the form of buried treasure. So I left Arizona and went treasure huntin' up at Taos, New Mexico. You ever been up there, boy? Course you ain't. I keep forgettin' you ain't been out of West Texas. Well, Taos is one of them adobe towns full of Mexicans, Indians, gringos, and nutty artists. A feller had sold me this treasure map and told me to look up a *bruja*. You know what that is? Course you don't. Well, it's a sort of fortuneteller and witch combined."

He gave that tomato can full of money a good rattle and went on, "Well, I found her. Yessir, by jingos, I found her all right, and she said the map was true and the treasure was buried there, but a lady had built a house over it. So we went to this lady and she said she could tell by the map her bedroom was right smack over the treasure, and if we'd split we could tear up the floor and dig it up. Well, I tore up the floor. The *bruja* said, 'dig there,' and I dug. I had dirt piled all over the place. Pretty soon the *bruja* said, 'The devils are at work and they have caused us to dig in the wrong place.' Well, sir, she grabbed a poker hanging by the fireplace and rammed it about three inches into the dry hard ground and said, 'There! There it is!' Hell's fire I stood right there and pulled on that poker, trying to get it out of the way so I could dig. And the harder I pulled, the deeper in the ground it went. When it went out of sight I naturally couldn't hold on any longer. Now I ain't the kind of feller to scare easy, but I broke into a run and I ain't been back to that insane town since. Ain't hunted much treasure either."

"What about the floor?" I asked.

"I never did write to find out."

He would have gone on for two hours telling me yarns, but I suddenly remembered how hungry I was so I said, "Let's go over to the café and buy us a big dinner. I'm starvin'."

"Now there you go, not thinkin' again. We just can't go in there like this. If they catch us faking this blind act, to jail we go. Come here," he said, and ducked my head under a water faucet and washed me off. Then he pulled out a dirty comb and slicked my hair back. "Take off your shirt and turn it wrong side out. Now," he said, "you can go over to the store and get us some grub. Hell's fire you look just like the mayor's son. I don't hardly know you myself."

He handed me a list and I walked over to the store. I got cheese and crackers, a loaf of bread and four cans of sardines for tonight. Then I got us another big bag of those dried apricots and a slab of cured bacon. We could take these along with us and they wouldn't spoil. Besides we had lots of money left. I went all the way and bought Boggs two new plugs of tobacco and me a Hershey bar.

We rode out to our camp that night with Boggs singing "When the Saints Go Marching Off," just chewing and spitting between notes.

Six

THE NEXT day we just loafed around and watched the horses graze. It was the first time we'd been sure of eating for over one day at a time.

Boggs said, "Boy, you ain't wrote a line to your mother since we've been gone."

"She don't expect me to."

"That's right, boy, she don't. But that ain't keepin' her from hopin'. Now is it?"

"I reckon not," I said, getting scared again.

Boggs tore a piece of brown sack up and handed it to me along with a stub of pencil.

"I ain't never wrote a letter home," I said.

"Might as well start now," he said. "It ain't much work and it'll do your ma a lot of good. It'll even make *you* feel better. You can drop it in the mail when we ride through Ropesville."

Well I was out of arguments with this man Boggs, so I wrote my first letter home.

Dear Ma,

*I'm sending this letter just to you cause I expect **Pa is** gone off somewhere on a deal. He generally is. How is old Blue and her pups. I sure hope we can keep the brindle one. He's going to make a real keen rabbit dog. I can tell because the roof of his mouth is black. That there is a sure sign.*

Did the old red hen hatch her chicks yet? I hope she saves all of them so we'll have fried chicken this August.

Me and Boggs are making it just fine. Ever time he talks it's about something different. He kind of puzzles me.

Is the cow giving lots of milk? I bet her calf is fat. Are you going to try and can everthing in the garden like you did last year? Don't work too hard on the garden or the canning either.

This man Boggs is a funny feller. Sometimes I think he's the smartest man in the world and sometimes I think he's the dumbest. Are you getting any sewing done? Don't worry about patching my overalls for school. I just plain know we're going to get into Oklahoma with all these horses and make us rich. The horses are looking better.

Love,

Your son Dan

There was no question now, the horses were putting on good solid meat. I could tell by looking and I could tell by my sore hind end.

Ropesville had been good to us. We fed regular — regular for us, and the horses had done the same. Besides, we had some money in Boggs' pocket and some sowbelly and pork and beans in that pack. Things looked better all the time. That's what I was thinking about five miles out of Ropesville when I noticed the old gray horse throw his head back and stop. The horse in front of him had also stopped and was holding up one foot.

"Boggs," I yelled, "come here. Something's wrong with this bay horse."

Boggs reined back and we both dismounted. He picked up the forefoot and examined it. I could see it was a bad cut.

"He stepped on a piece of glass, looks like to me," Boggs said.

I walked back a few steps and sure enough there was a broken bottle.

"What do we do?" I asked, fearing what he'd tell me.

"There ain't a thing to do, boy. With the best of care this horse is going to be lame for a month or more. The frog is cut deep. We'll just have to leave him. I'll go up here to this farm and see what we can work out."

He was gone maybe ten minutes before he returned with a man. They both looked at the foot again.

Boggs said, "He's yours if you'll doctor him."

"I'll give it a try," the man said looking worried.

"Now listen," Boggs said, "soon as you ease him up to the barn throw some diluted kerosene on it. It might burn him a little but it'll take a lot of soreness out quick. Then make a poultice out of wagon grease and churn butter. The grease will keep the flies from getting to it and the butter will take out the fever."

"I'll give it a try," the man said again.

I wanted to say that my hind end could still use some of

that butter, but I felt too bad about the horse. Now we were falling short on delivering the goods and we had a long way to go yet.

"Let's git goin', boy."

I rode along now feeling blue and upset. After a while I thought I might as well try to cheer myself up so I started trying to guess what the fanciest present this side of the pearly gates would be. Maybe Boggs would get me a new hat. Or even better a new pair of boots. I'd never had a new pair of boots — just old brogan shoes. It was a disgrace. Why, I'd be thirteen my next birthday. And that birthday was tomorrow according to the calendar in that Ropesville café.

All of a sudden Boggs rode back. "Look there, boy, there's Lubbock."

"I was there once," I said blowing up a mite. But I was really too little to remember. The tall buildings stuck up out of the plains so's you could see them for miles around. "Man, that must be a big town."

"Naw, it ain't nothin', boy. You should see Denver, or San Francisco or Mexico City."

"You been all them places?"

"Hell's fire yes, and a lot more besides."

I still wasn't going to give up on Lubbock. "How many people you reckon lives there?"

"Oh, maybe twenty-five thousand."

I whistled.

"See that building? The tallest one?"

"Yeah."

"Well, that's a hotel. I still got a suitcase in there. One

time I was driftin' through here and went broke as a pullet bone. I figgered and figgered how to get out of that hotel without paying."

"You was thinkin'," I volunteered.

"By jingos, you're right, I sure was. Well I took a shirt and put all my other clothes, all my shaving equipment and some crooked dice I happened to have with me, in this shirt. Then I tied it up in a bundle so's it would look like a bundle of dirty laundry. As I stepped out into the hall one end of that shirt came open and dice and razors and all sorts of stuff fell right out on the floor. A porter and two maids just stood there and stared while I gathered it all up and tied it back tight. That was where they let the hotel down. Before they could get to a service elevator to squeal on me, I was already down three flights of stairs and asking the desk man where the nearest laundry was. Well now, once ole Boggs got outside I was gone. That little Ford car just purred me right out of town."

"Ain't that cheatin', Boggs?"

"Why, Lord, no. What's the matter with you, boy? That's what you call tradin'. I left them a sure-enough good, empty two-dollar suitcase for a week's rent and feed."

The closer we got to Lubbock the more my eyes bugged. It sure was a whopper. We skirted around the east side of town next to the Texas Tech campus. Boggs pulled up.

"Here's a nice little pasture to hole up in. I've got to get on into town and do a little shoppin'. You'll have to stay here with the horses, boy. Part of my shoppin' you wouldn't understand anyway."

Well, just as we were unloading the pack mule, we heard a truck coming. There were two men in it and one of them said, "What the hell you think you're doin' turnin' a whole herd of horses in my pasture? I'm a notion to impound 'em."

Well, my little skinny heart was tearing my ribs out. That was all we needed to fail Papa completely.

"Why, my good sir," said Boggs, "let it be my pleasure to inform you kind gentlemen that we have merely paused a fleeting moment in our travels to relieve for an instant the burden of this fine pack mule. I am a preacher of the gospel. Myself and my young apprentice are heading north — our eventual destiny to be deepest Alaska. There we intend to bring about a revival of the Eskimos that will shake the northern world. Our horses we shall trade for reindeer upon our arrival. There are some things a reindeer can do that are beyond the capabilities of the American horse. Suffice it to say that with another moment's kind indulgence we shall wend our way over the great horizon to far distant and untamed shores."

One of the men just stared puzzled, the other one said, "Well, I don't know about that."

"And what, my beloved fellow inhabitant of this celestial globe, can I inform you of?"

"Jist git out, that's all, jist git out." They drove away mumbling under their breaths.

"Well, we shall skirt on around town, my boy. There's a canyon full of grass to the north of town. Yellow House Canyon by name. We shall perhaps find a better sanctuary there."

I was wishing he would shut up that silly talk, and quit practicing on me. Hell's fire, I was ole Dan.

It took us another hour to skirt town and sure enough there was a nice little canyon with lots of grass. We pulled up into a little offset and pitched camp.

Boggs said, "Now get a good rest. There's plenty of grub for a change. I'll see you afterwhile." He rode off on a black, leading the pack mule. I had me a nice meal. Worried awhile about losing the horse and finally fell to sleep.

It was getting somewhere close to ten o'clock the next morning when I heard a heck of a yell. I looked up and there came Boggs down the other side of the canyon. He kept yelling and singing. And that mule was having a hard time keeping up with him. There was stuff hanging all over the pack.

"Happy Birthday, Dear Dan'l, Happy Birthday to You." He was really singing it out and swaying in the saddle till I was certain he'd fall off. He jumped off his horse and shook me by the hand so hard I thought he was going to unsocket my arm. He lifted the jug from the pack and said, "Here's to you, Dan'l, and a happy birthday it's goin' to be. I got no more earaches, Dan'l. Whooooopp-eee! Happy birthday to you!" He ran over to the pack and grabbed a secondhand No. 3 washtub. "Gather the wood, boy. Gather the wood."

I knew better than to do anything else. But since the mesquite was thin here I had a devil of a time keeping him supplied.

He dumped a ten-pound sack of flour in the tub. A five-pound sack of sugar followed. Then he threw in a can of baking powder, and I don't know what else. He wouldn't let me stay to watch. Said it was going to be a surprise. I watched for a minute from off a ways. He ran down to a little muddy spring with a rusty bucket and got some water. Then he stirred it all up with a mesquite limb.

Well, when I got back with my next load of wood, the fire was blazing under this tub, and he said, "Here's your surprise, boy. It's a chocolate cake. Now what boy on this earth ever had a chocolate birthday cake like that?"

I had to admit that I doubted if there had ever been such an event take place before. Well, I kept carrying the wood. And he threw it on the fire and stirred. After a while the cake started rising. He kept shushing me to walk quiet.

"Hawww, boy, watch your step, you'll make this cake drop."

Well I figger that nine hundred buffalo could have stampeded right past and that cake would not have dropped. In fact it rose up in the air about eighteen inches above the rim of that tub and just ran out in all directions. Boggs had taken his earache medicine and bedded down.

For a while I thought I needed his help when it looked as if the cake would fill up the canyon, but when it finally cooled and I took a bite I was real glad he was asleep. I choked for thirty minutes. After I got finished choking, I hauled most of it off and fed it to the magpies. I didn't want to hurt his feelings. I should have had some consideration though for the magpies, but in those days I was just a growing boy.

Seven

WE WORKED our way north of Lubbock through country spotted with cotton fields, sorghum — thick and heavy leaved, and here and there the brown stubble rectangle of an oat patch already cut and stored. On past Plainview we got into some grassland again, and that's where something happened.

We were moving out of a small draw through some cutbanks when the old gray horse pulled out of line reaching for a special clump of grass. I reined over to the edge of the sharply sloping cutbank and yelled "Haaarr" at him. Just as I did, my horse bolted to the side and I went down hard against the ground. I was sort of off balance laying on the slope of the cutbank. I reached up to get hold of a thick clump of grass to raise myself, when I heard the rattle. The snake lay coiled on a level patch. That's what had boogered my horse.

We looked each other right in the eye. I strained my

left arm where I held the grass clump. The snake struck out right at my head, but he was short an inch or two. Now, I *was* in a fix. I could tell the grass roots would give way if I put any more weight on them. If they did, I'd slide right on top the snake.

His little black eyes looked at me over his darting tongue, and suddenly they seemed as big as light bulbs. And that forked tongue dropping in and out was nothing to make me happier. I could feel the sweat all over, and a ringing in my head. For a minute I nearly fainted. Then for some reason I thought of Papa and how he was depending on me. If I panicked and got snake-bit the whole thing would be blown up. Everybody's hopes would be done in. But I didn't know what to do. If Boggs just knew, but of course, he couldn't. He couldn't see me. I'd just have to hold on as long as I could, and maybe the snake would go away. It wasn't advancing, but it wasn't backing up either. It just lay there coiled, its head in striking position, shaking those rattlers a hundred miles a minute. I kept feeling like I was sliding right into those fangs. I couldn't move but just the same I pressured my belly into the dirt hoping to hold.

Then I heard the voice coming, easy and sure. "Don't move, Dan boy. Boy, you hear me, don't you? Well, keep still now. Just a little longer, boy."

I didn't even twitch an eyeball. I saw him crawl into my range of vision. He had a stick held out in front of him and he was kind of humming the same note over and over and twisting the end of the stick in a slow circle. Closer, closer, hum, hum. The stick circled near the

snake's arched neck. Nothing but the tongue and the rattlers moved now. Then the head shot out and Boggs
scooped the snake onto the end of the stick and hurled
him way down to the bottom of the draw.

I was paralyzed another moment. Then I leaped up
screaming, "Kill him! Kill him, Boggs!"

Boggs sat down beside me, and said, "Now, just calm
down, boy. You're fine and the snake's fine."

"Ain't you goin' to kill him?"

"Lord a Mercy no, I ain't goin' to kill him. Why, that
poor old snake's in the same war we are."

"War?"

"Sure enough, boy, he's fightin' those pack rats harder'n
we are."

I forgot all about the loss of the horse, and when I
found out that Amarillo was a bigger town than Lubbock
I even forgot about the rattlesnake for a while.

I did wish I could go uptown and see all the sights, but
Boggs said that would come for me soon enough; besides we had to stay on the march and take care of our
horses now.

Eight

BETWEEN the towns of Amarillo and Dumas, Texas, runs the Canadian River. We drove our horses along the highway until we spotted the long, narrow cement bridge crossing it.

Boggs threw up his hand and stopped the horses. He rode back to talk to me.

"I don't believe we better try to take the horses across the bridge. We're goin' to block too much traffic. And besides we've got to have a permit, as well as the highway patrol to watch both ends. It's too late to get either now. We only have one choice, boy; that's bend the horses back to a gate and ride east down the river till we find a crossing."

This we proceeded to do.

I could see the storm sweeping toward us from the west and north. It must have been over a hundred miles in width. We had to cross the Canadian before it hit. This river is nothing to play with. It is full of quicksand and bogholes, and when it rains heavily to the west a front of water drops down out of New Mexico and West Texas with great force and speed.

Most of the time, though, the Canadian is a quiet river. Many places in its bed are as wide as the Mississippi, but during dry spells only a few small, red, muddy streams trickle through its bottom. Cottonwoods break the tree-less plain along its banks, and cattle come to water from it for hundreds of miles up and down. Wild turkey, quail, coyotes, antelopes and many other kinds of wild game love the Canadian. But to man it is always treacherous.

For ten or twelve miles on each side are the sand hills — thousands upon thousands of tiny, rough, ever-chang-ing hills of sand — spotted with sage, shinnery, mes-quite and yucca. The yucca was green now, and the pods were soon to open their beautiful, milk-white blooms.

We rode hard, pushing the horses through and around over the sand. The old gray could only be moved so fast. So that I was constantly having to yell and crowd the poor thing. But he did his best for me.

There was no sun as the huge cloud blanket moved on towards us and shadowed the land. The lightning was cracking so fast now that the thunder was a continuous roar, never letting up, but varying its sound like rolling waves. Even without the sun it was hot — sure enough hot. The horses were lathered white. And my almost healed-over hind end was sweated to the back of my mount. The Canadian looked fifty miles wide to me but was actually only about three eighths where Boggs finally chose to cross.

I crowded the old gray down into the clay and sand of the bottom. There were tracks where a cowboy had crossed here. The forefront of the storm clouds was moving up over us now. I kept glancing up the river, fearing that wall of water I knew had to be moving upon us from the west. The wind was intense and the horses' manes and tails blew out almost parallel with the ground. We struck a few shallow bogholes where our mounts went through to the hard clay underneath.

Way up the river bottom I could see the rain reaching out into the banks and I knew a head of water was racing right along with the storm. I saw a small tornado drop down out of the sky for the ground and then return like a hand reaching out of a shawl to pick up something. Several writhing snakes of cloud broke loose in torment. I could hear the roar of the rain above the thunder now and its chorus — the river.

I almost panicked and left the old gray horse. More than anything I wanted to get out of the river bottom and up to the banks above the cottonwoods. Even if there was a tornado there. And there *was* one just beyond. I could see the inverted funnel ripping at the earth. Black. Mad.

Now we were on a huge sandbar that carried all the way to the bank. There was no turning back. There was no detour. Underneath the slight crust of its top was quicksand. Deep and deadly. The sand shook and quivered like Jello. The bank was nearer now.

The old gray stumbled and the extra force against the ground broke the crust. He went in up to his belly. I rode up beside him and pulled at his mane. My horse was sweated and excited and almost jumped out from under me. For a moment I thought the quicksand would get him. The more I pulled, the more the old gray fought, the deeper he sank. I was crying and begging the old horse now. And it wasn't just because it meant another loss to Papa, but it was a loss to me. He was my friend, this old horse.

And then I heard Boggs. He was riding back across the bar. "Git, boy! Look!"

I saw the terrible churning wall of dirty, red water racing at us. He slapped me hard up the side of my head and said, "Ride!"

I rode on by the old gray and I saw his nostrils almost tearing his face. His eyes rolled back as he sunk to his withers. In his eyes there was an acceptance along with the terror.

We rode up on the bank as the rain hit us harder and the edge of the tornado squalled on by. I got one glimpse of the old gray straining to throw his head above the river's blood, and then he was gone.

It rained for two hours and then the sun came out. We were very cold and very wet. It didn't even bother me. The river would be up all night. We gathered our horses and moved on across the sand hills. I didn't look back.

Nine

I HAD A numb feeling as we rode along. We were getting into the last stages of our drive, and we were two horses short. It was just plain awful to let Papa down. I was sick thinking about it.

We reached the edge of Dumas, Texas, on a Sunday. We knew that was the day, for the churches were filled with singing and shouting. I watched Boggs up ahead. I could almost see him quiver, he wanted to get in there and go to preaching so bad. He raised his hand and stopped the horses. They milled about and started grazing on somebody's lawn.

He rode back to me. "Boy," he said, "it's takin' all my willpower to stay out of that church. I'd like to go in and talk that Reverend into ten minutes with Boggs. There's a lot of sinners in there and they think they're saved, but ten minutes later I'd have 'em lined up and headin' for a baptizin'."

It sounded like he wanted me to say Go ahead. So I said, "I'll watch the horses, Boggs, if you want to go in."

"That's a magnanimous gesture, boy, but I reckon we've got to do somethin' about replenishin' this herd of horses. We just cain't let your papa down. And besides, your ma is staying back there worrying herself sick about the mortgages and all that. Now the way I got it figgered is this: These little West Texas towns all have baseball teams. Today is bound to be Sunday. There'll be a ball game around here somewhere."

Well he was right. We found the baseball grounds out on the edge of town in a big opening. We turned our horses loose on the grass and rode over where a man was dragging the field down with a tractor and scraper.

"Yes sir, there's going to be a ball game," he said, taking a chew of the tobacco Boggs offered him. "Spearman, Texas, will be here in just a little while. They've got a good team but we've got a better one."

"Is that so?" Boggs said. "What kind of pitchers you got?"

"One good 'un, and one bad 'un."

"Sounds about right."

I was sure puzzled about Boggs' interest in baseball, but since we were going to graze the horses awhile we might as well have a little fun watching a baseball game.

The crowd began to gather early. They came by truck, car, wagon and horseback. The teams began to warm up their pitchers and everybody was getting excited. Seems like this was an old rivalry.

I followed Boggs around till he found the manager of the Spearman team. This man also chewed tobacco, but when Boggs offered him a chew he reared back and looked out over his monstrous cornfed belly and said, "That ain't my brand."

Boggs said, "How much would it be worth to you to win this game?"

"Well in money, not much. I only got five dollars bet on it. But in personal satisfaction, my friend, it would be a strain for a millionaire to pay off."

I could tell the way he talked, they were going to get along.

"Did you ever hear of Booger Boggs who played for the East Texas League?" Boggs asked.

"Sure. Everybody's heard of Booger Boggs. Why?"

"That's me."

"Ahhhh," and he started laughing and laughing. "You're jist a farmhand. Maybe a bronc rider, by the looks of them legs."

Boggs was quiet for once. He let the manager finish out his laugh then he said, "Can you catch a ball?"

"Sure. I *am* the Spearman catcher."

"Well, go get your mitt and get me a glove and ball, my dear associate."

While the unbelieving fat man went after the equipment, Boggs started warming up his arm, swinging it around and around.

"Now, son," he said to me, and I knew he was really going to get serious because of the "son" bit, "this old arm ain't in much shape and it'll never be any good after today, but I just want you to know I'm going to give'r all I got."

"You goin' to pitch?"

"You just wait and see."

He threw a few soft ones at the manager and then he let one fly that purty nearly tore the catcher's arm off. I knew he was going to get his chance. He went around and started a few conversations.

"You folks from Dumas don't know when you're beat. I'm goin' to sack you boys out today." As usual when they looked at Boggs everybody just laughed and laughed. That's what he wanted them to do.

One of the sporting boys said, "If you're goin' to pitch I'd like to lay a little money on the line. Now, if you ain't just a blowhard, why don't you put your money where your mouth is?"

"Well now, I ain't got no money, my dear compatriots, but I've got something better," and he swept a long arm at our horses grazing off aways. I'll bet any four of that fine bunch against any two of yours."

One man got so carried away he said, "I'll bet my good wagon and team with the grain and laying mash that's in it and a box of groceries to boot."

That was the only bet Boggs called. They shook hands and had plenty of witnesses.

The game started. I watched Boggs fan three Dumas men in a row. Then Spearman got a man on base. The next two up for our side struck out and the Dumas catcher threw our man out trying to steal second. Then Boggs fanned another and two grounded out to shortstop. And right on into the sixth inning scoreless. Then I could tell Boggs' arm was weakening. A Dumas batter swatted a long, high fly that should have been an easy out in left field. The fielder just plain dropped it. The man scored standing up.

Well, Boggs took off his glasses, pulled out his shirttail, and went to cleaning that lens. He took his time about it. Everybody was wondering what difference it could make if he cleaned a glass that fit over a blind eye. So did I.

The Dumas fans were naturally rawhiding him quite a bit and the Spearman team was getting uneasy. I watched him closely. He was up to something. I knew that no matter what Boggs was, I'd never see another anywhere like him. Come to think of it that's a whole bunch to say about any man. He was at *least* three different men and maybe a dozen.

When he got through cleaning his glasses he slowly put them back on. Then he took off his hat and his glove and held the ball high in the air. And he shouted so that everybody quieted down.

"Lord, up there in the great universe, heed my call. Lord, I'm goin' to ask you to put some devil on this ball. Just let me use him a little. I want a devil curve and a devil drop and a devil fast ball, and I'll guarantee you that the end of the game will belong to you, Lord. What I want is victory. Now I know you heard me, your honor, Lord. So it's up to me. And if I don't win this game bring a bolt of lightning down upon my unworthy head and burn me to a cinder. Amen and thanks."

I looked up in the cloudless sky and thought that even the Lord would have to strain to get lightning out of that blue sky.

He pulled his hat back on tight, picked up the glove

and ball, squinted out that glassless rim, took a big spit of tobacco, and let fly. No matter what happened to this game it was quite a sight to see him pitch. Those runover high-heeled boots, bib overalls, and that old floppy hat sure were different to say just a little.

That ball whistled in there so solid and fast the batter fell down hitting at it. Boggs didn't waste any time now, just wound up once and let fly. The ball broke in a curve and the batter nearly broke his neck fishing for it. The next one was a drop — breaking sharp and clean. The umpire yelled "Strike!" and thumbed him out. A great roar went up from the Spearman rooters.

After that it was a walk-in. Boggs had shot his wad on those three pitches. He was faking his way now. The spirit of the home team was broken. The Spearman players started a seventh-inning rally and the way they batted I could have been pitching for them and they would have won.

The game wound up nine to one and we had us a team of horses, one of which was a mare with a colt by her side, a wagon, a lot of feed, plus a big box of groceries.

Boggs was carrying his arm at his side. It was obvious he'd never pitch again, not even for fun.

Ten

WHEN WE headed out of Dumas the next day I was sure a happy kid. As soon as Boggs was up ahead where he couldn't see I just plain let loose and bawled. After that I felt fine.

Now our only problem, if we were lucky, was the time. We were a half day behind. At the same time we couldn't push the horses too hard or it would gaunt them and the buyers wouldn't pay enough. I drove our wagon with my saddle horse tied behind. We'd taken the pack off the mule and so we all moved out pretty good.

Wheat country sprung up all around now. The plowed fields contrasted to the rich green of the sorghum. There was a zillion miles of sky all around. The farms and ranches looked peaceful and prosperous, but every little bit I could see where the drought still showed its fangs — fences buried beneath drifting sand, fields barren, and cut to clay beds. But this new idea of contour plowing, so

the land wouldn't wash, was sure enough helping. I
didn't like to remember the dust that came and choked
and killed and desecrated the land like the earth had suddenly turned to brown sugar. I liked to think about the
green growing things. But I was young and I know I'd
never have appreciated the wet years without the dry
ones.

Night and day became almost the same. We didn't
sleep or stop much and when we pulled into Stratford,
Texas, in the upper Panhandle, we were dead tired. We
camped about four or five miles from town. It was so
thinly populated we could see only one farmhouse close by.

We ate, turned the horses loose to graze, all except the
one we left tied to the wagon eating grain, and went to
sleep.

As usual Boggs was up before the sun. "Go drive the
horses over close while I fix breakfast. That way we'll save
a few minutes."

I saddled up and rode out through the mesquite. I was
surprised the horses weren't nearby because the grass
was good everywhere and they like to stay fairly close to
the grain. I tracked them a ways and blamed if they
hadn't walked right up to this farmhouse. There they all
were in a corral. I felt a hurt come in my belly. A hurt of
fear. Those horses durn sure hadn't penned themselves,
and we were on somebody's private land. I didn't have
long to wait, before I found out whose.

He sat on a big plow horse holding a shotgun, and
spoke in a mean voice, "Thought you'd be around directly.
Well now, boy, where's your pa?"

"At Guymon, Oklahoma."

"Guymon, huh? Well now, ain't that interestin'. What's he doin' off up there?"

"Waitin' for me," I said swallering and feeling the tears start to burn. I choked them back.

"Who's helpin' you with these?" He motioned the shotgun at the horses. He was a short man but broad and big-bellied. He wore a tiny hat that just barely sat on top of his head and his mouth hung loose around his fat face. I couldn't see his eyes, just holes in the fat where they were.

"I reckon you know you were trespassin'?"

"Yes sir."

"Well, cain't you read?"

"Yes sir."

"Well, then how come you didn't heed my 'posted' sign?"

"Didn't see it."

"Well" (he started nearly every sentence with "well"), "I'll tell you one thing young man, you'll look the next time you come around my place. You got any money?"

"No, sir."

"Well, now ain't that too bad. I'm just going to have to ride into town, get the marshal, and we'll have to have a sale to justify the damage to my land. Five dollars a head, that's the law. If you cain't pay, I take the horses."

"But we ain't got anything else, no way to live . . ."

He interrupted, "Well, you should've been thinkin' about that when you rode on my place and started destroying my grass."

"Please."

"Too late for that, sonny."

I had to stall for time. I said, "Look, mister, I know you're goin' to take my horses, but first, before we go, could I have a drink of water?"

"Ain't no harm in that," he said. "But hurry it up. I ain't got all day."

I went over to the horse trough and drank just as long as I could. I thought I saw something moving out near our camp.

"Hurry it up, sonny. Get on your horse and let's go."

I walked up to my horse and picked his hind foot up. I glanced under his belly and I could see Boggs snaking along from one yucca clump to another, and it sure looked like he was *eating* yucca blooms. The damn fool was going to get himself shot sneaking up this way. My horse heard him and pitched his ears in that direction.

"Here, sonny, what you doin'? That horse ain't lame. Now get up on there before I give you a load of this here buckshot."

I got up on my horse just as Boggs raised up and broke into a wild, arm-waving, screaming run right for us. The froth was streaming out both sides of his mouth. His one eye gleamed right at us just like a wild man's.

That horse under that man with the shotgun just snorted and jumped right straight up in the air. When his hoofs hit the ground, there wasn't anybody on his back. That feller came down hard and the shotgun blew both barrels. The horses and mules broke out of the corral and ran back towards our camp snorting and blowing to beat seventy-five.

I finally got my horse calmed down and when I did I saw Boggs sitting on top of the feller who once had a shotgun. He reached over and tapped him up beside the head with a rock. The man slept. Boggs got some rope from the barn and tied him up.

"Go round up the horses," he said as he stuffed the man's mouth full of shirttail.

I soon had them cornered, and tempting them with a little oats in a bucket, they finally followed me over to the wagon. By then Boggs was back. We caught our team, hooked them up and got to hell out of the country as fast as we could.

"Boggs," I said, "we've got to go back. We cain't leave that man tied up out in the hot sun all day. It'll kill him. Besides he might starve to death before anybody comes by to see him, as ornery as he is."

"Don't fret, boy. I turned him loose."

"Loose?" Well, I worried again. "Reckon he'll have the law after us right away."

"No, it'll take him two days to walk to his nearest neighbor's."

"How come?"

"Just before I turned him loose I sort of twisted his ankle a little."

"Why, that's plumb cruel."

"No such thing, boy. That ankle was clear out of shape. Always had been. From the looks it growed that way. I just put it back where it belonged."

What could a kid like me say about a thing like that?

We rode on now through the day and into the night,

and then again. We let the horses have twelve hours on grass and a big bait of grain just before we crossed the state line into the Oklahoma Panhandle. The last lap now.

This strip had once belonged to Texas until around 1850 when they sold it to the United States, as part of the territory including New Mexico, Colorado, Wyoming and Kansas. It had been known as the "strip" and "no man's land" until 1890 when the Strip was made a part of the Oklahoma Territory.

It was part of the great plains we'd just come across. These vast regions shot northward all the way through the Dakotas, Montana and into Canada. My hind end felt like we had covered our part of it.

Late in the afternoon of the next day we spotted Guymon. We unrolled the map out of the oilcloth wrapper and studied it.

"The sale is tomorrow at noon," Boggs said. "That means we need these horses in there at ten o'clock like your pappy said. The buyers like to look before the biddin' starts."

"We're late," I said feeling cold and weak.

"No sir, we turn up here about a mile and then it's nine more northeast from there. If we ride way in the night we can make it."

"But the horses'll be gaunted down."

"No, we'll feed them a good bait of grain and give them till eight in the morning to graze. If we find grass where we stop we'll be all right."

"If we don't?"

"Like I said, son, there's risks in everything. That's where the fun comes in life."

"Let's git goin'," I said.

We pushed the horses on. They didn't like it and kept trying to graze in the bar ditches of the country lanes. We made them move. I left it up to Boggs to lead, hoping hard he was going in the right direction. For a long time we could see the orange light of the farmhouses sprinkled off across the prairie and once in a while a car light moved in the night. Then all the lights were gone except those of the stars and a half-moon. It was enough. I nearly went to sleep several times, but I'd wake up just before falling off the wagon. It seemed like we'd ridden a hundred years to me. My body was still working but my mind had long ago gone numb.

Then there was Boggs. "Take a nap, son. There's plenty of grass for the horses right along the road. I'll stay up and watch 'em."

I crawled in the wagon bed fully intending to sleep an hour or so and then relieve Boggs. It didn't work like that. The sun was up and warm when he woke me.

"Get up, boy, and let's have another look at the map."

I raised up fumbling sleepily for it.

"Here it is!" he cried. "Here it is! Look, two dry lake beds, then take the first turn to the left for one mile. Look," he pointed up ahead and there were two dry lake beds. A tingling came over me. Boggs handed me a cup of coffee and said, "Just a minute and I'll fix you some bacon."

"Don't want any."

"Let's git goin', Dan boy," he said, grinning all over.

It took us a while to get hooked up and on the move. The colt bounced saucily along beside the wagon. The horses were full and although they weren't fat, they had lots of good solid meat on them. They were strong, tough, and so was I. I was burned brown as a Comanche warrior and my hind end had turned to iron.

Papa saw us coming and headed down to meet us in his old Ford. He jumped out and said, "Howdy, fellers. Why look at Dan. Boy, you've growed a whole nickel's worth. Have any trouble, Boggs?"

"No sir, not a bit."

I didn't tell Papa any different. Besides he had such faith in us he didn't count the horses. If he had he'd have found there was one extra.

The sale went over big for us. Uncle Jock really got his best chant going. When it was all over Papa had cleared over twenty dollars a head on the horses and nearly thirty on the mules. Ma could rest easy and go ahead and plan her garden for the next spring. Papa gave me three whole dollars to spend just any way I pleased.

Soon as we got home I went over to Starvation to drink a few orange soda pops and get my present from Boggs. He didn't show up the first day and he didn't show up for a whole week. I was getting a trifle worried but figured maybe he'd had to go plumb up to Lubbock to find me the new pair of boots. I'd made up my mind that's what he'd give me for using my saddle.

Well, on the eighth day I ran into him coming out of Johnson's Grocery, and said, "Hi, Boggs."

"Well, howdy yourself, Dan. How've you been?"

"Fine," I said. "Did you get me the present you promised?"

"Just a minute, boy," he said, and walked back in the store. He came out with a nickel pecan bar. I took it. He said again, "Just a minute, boy," and went back in the store.

I figured he must be getting my present wrapped up pretty for me, so I hunkered down on the porch and started eating my candy bar. It sure was thoughtful of Boggs to feed me this candy while I was waiting. I'd eaten about half of it before I noticed the funny taste. I took a close look. That candy bar was full of worms. Live ones.

I got up and went in the store. I walked on towards the back figuring Boggs was behind the meat counter. Then I saw this table that said: ALL CANDY ON THIS TABLE PRICED ONE CENT. There were lots of those wormy pecan bars among them.

He wasn't at the meat counter and I asked, "Mr. Johnson, do you know where Boggs went?"

He said, "No, I don't. He walked out the back door."

Well it finally glimmered in my little brain what had happened. I got mad. Real mad. I got me a board and I went all over town looking. I was going to knock his head clean off if I found him. It got dark. I waited at the back of the pool hall looking through a window for him. I waited till it closed. I waited till the whole town closed. I was in such a rage I nearly died.

I never found Boggs. In fact, I never saw him again. I don't know where he came from and I don't know where he drifted to. But by jingos I sort of miss him. After all he *was* my pardner.